Sunrise behind

Léo Malet was born
formal education an
enragée' in Montmar
contributed to various magazines: *L'Insurgé, Le Journal de l'Homme aux sandales* . . . He had various jobs: office worker, ghost writer, manager of a fashion magazine, cinema extra, newspaper seller . . .

From 1930 to 1940 he belonged to the Surrealist Group and was a close friend of André Breton, René Magritte and Yves Tanguy. During that time he published several collections of poetry.

In 1943, inspired by the American writers Raymond Chandler and Dashiel Hammett, he created Nestor Burma, the Parisian private detective whose first mystery *120, rue de la Gare* was an instant success and marked the beginning of a new era in French detective fiction.

More than sixty novels were to follow over the next twenty years. Léo Malet won the 'Grand Prix de la Littérature policière' in 1947 and the 'Grand Prix de l'Humour Noir' in 1958 for his series 'Les Nouveaux Mystères de Paris', each of which is set in a different *arrondissement*. *Sunrise behind the Louvre*, depicting the 1st *arrondissement*, was first published in 1954.

Léo Malet lives in Châtillon, just south of Paris.

Also by Léo Malet in Pan Books

The Rats of Montsouris
120 rue de la Gare
Mission to Marseilles

Léo Malet

Sunrise behind the Louvre

translated from the French by Barbara Bray
General editor: Barbara Bray

Pan Books
London, Sydney and Auckland

First published in France 1954 by Ed. R. Laffont, Paris

as *Le Soleil naît derrière le Louvre*

Published in France 1981 by Editions Fleuve Noir

This edition first published in Great Britain 1991 by
Pan Books Ltd, Cavaye Place, London SW10 9PG

9 8 7 6 5 4 3 2 1

© Léo Malet 1954

This English translation © Aramos 1991

ISBN 0 330 31850 0

Typeset by Macmillan Production Limited

Printed in England by Clays Ltd, St Ives plc

This book is sold subject to the condition that it shall not,
by way of trade or otherwise, be lent, re-sold, hired out,
or otherwise circulated without the publisher's prior consent
in any form of binding or cover other than that in which
it is published and without a similar condition including this
condition being imposed on the subsequent purchaser

Contents

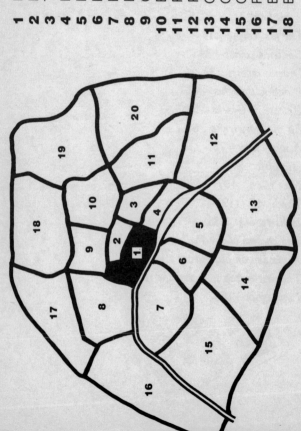

1 Louvre
2 Bourse
3 Temple
4 Hôtel-de-Ville
5 Panthéon
6 Luxembourg
7 Palais-Bourbon
8 Elysée
9 Opéra
10 Entrepôt
11 Popincourt
12 Reuilly
13 Gobelins
14 Observatoire
15 Grenelle/Vaugirard
16 Passy / Auteuil
17 Batignolles-Monceau
18 Butte-Montmartre

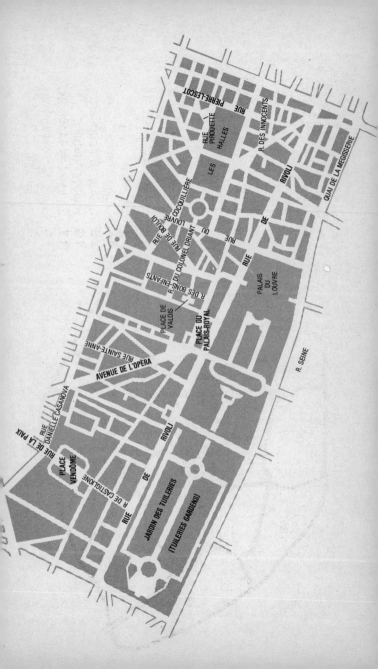

1 A bit low

The one hanging around the entrance to the Métro hadn't been too badly brought up.

She said, 'Good evening, monsieur,' as I went past.

I replied, 'Good evening, madame,' and walked on. She wasn't the one I was looking for.

I turned into the rue des Lavandières-Sainte-Opportune.

A gust of rain caught me off guard. It seemed to come from the direction of the Law Courts, crouching dimly on the other side of the river with their towers pricked up like ears. I clutched at my hat just in time, and reflected that I'd be better off going home to bed.

Quite a mild night for January, but January just the same, and I preferred my cold showers in the summer. I kept telling myself I was more or less on duty, but I wasn't convinced. If I wanted to nab Louis Lheureux I need only wait till he went back to his hotel in the rue de Valois. It would be easier to make him see reason if I picked him up lowering brandies at a bar, but it wasn't absolutely necessary. Nor was there any sense, in this weather, in trying to trail him to his lady friends or checking out where he might go to eat. And yet . . And yet I enjoyed having a roam through the streets . . . They weren't too chilly, for January.

I gripped my pipe in my teeth, lowered my head like a racing cyclist, and headed for the shelter of the rue Jean-Lantier.

There, a few months earlier, a blonde by the name of Gaby had paced up and down dutifully between the entrances to the various hotels. She might still be there.

The street was a bit lighter than a railway tunnel, and I could see a couple of figures coming and going in the gloom. The first one leapt on me as if I were the Aga Khan in person, but she wasn't a blonde as far as I could see. At least, not an aggressively shiny platinum blonde like the one I had in mind.

'Isn't Gaby around?' I asked.

'I *am* Gaby,' answered a tired voice.

'But Gaby's a blonde.'

'Not any more, lovey. I changed the colour six months ago.'

'Can I have a proper look? I want to be sure I'm talking to the right person.'

'But I *am* Gaby, I tell you!'

And she was. I saw as much when I'd led her into the hallway of a seedy hotel and looked at her by the anaemic light of one fly-blown bulb. Her face was pretty, but it was anaemic too; sickly-looking, and neither young nor old.

'Satisfied?' she said.

'Yes.'

'So?'

'I just wanted to ask you something. Here's a thousand francs for your time.'*

* As the story takes place in 1954, all sums of money are in 'old' francs. (Ten old francs = one new – Translator's note)

She took the note without hesitation or comment and tucked it in her stocking. I had a glimpse of incipient varicose veins. That didn't surprise me. She was the kind of hooker who does more walking than lying down. She needed good shoes for that. But I seemed to remember her always wearing these open sandals. They couldn't have kept her feet very warm. It was further up, in the St Denis district, that the girls wore leather boots. And Gaby was practically shivering in her coat of cotton brushed to look like wool. It was further away still that you saw the high-flyers in furs. In the rue Caumartin. In another world.

'What do you want to know?' she asked.

'Don't you recognize me?' I said, pushing my hat back. She sighed.

'Oh, I see so many.'

If that was how she wanted it . . .

'My name's Nestor.'

'That's a funny name to go to bed with.'

'I manage. And I'm looking for a funny sort of guy. One of your clients. Louis, his name is, as I expect he's told you – he's a bit of a chatterbox. A middle-aged sucker from the provinces – from Limoges, as a matter of fact; he's always talking about it. He makes a trip up to town once a year. I took him under my wing last time – I make a very good nanny – and as I hear he's back again now, and I haven't been able to locate him, I was wondering . . . Do you know who I mean?'

She didn't have to think long.

'I believe so . . . A chap who always looks as if he's got some private joke?'

'That's him.'

'Oh yes, I remember him all right!'

'Why?'

'He's got nice manners, and he's not stingy. We could do with more like him! I don't care if you do say he's funny!'

'Has he been to see you this evening?'

'No,' she said with a sigh. 'Nor any other evening, lately.'

'Oh, well, too bad for all of us, eh? Thanks just the same, Gaby.'

'You're welcome.'

Her defeated eyes lingered on mine, wondering what it was all about, and whether my questions weren't going to lead to trouble. She had plenty of trouble already, with more bother from cops and the weather than from crowds of customers.

I was suddenly moved to pity.

It probably had something to do with the depressing surroundings. I'd been feeling a bit low ever since I got there. Nothing ever happens in that neighbourhood; it comes to life only at night – and for what? To fill bellies. It reeks of dead flesh and of vegetables wrenched from the earth. Not that things are any better in the daytime. Shops catering for labourers and skivvies. It's not till you get to the Place du Palais-Royal that the air gets less squalid – though the nearness of the Ministry of Finance soon puts paid to that slight improvement. And along by the river are the birds in cages. Whistling. Calling for help. Some hope! And the birds in the Tuileries Gardens aren't any freer. Their cage is merely a bit bigger and more grandiose. Honour is saved only by the pigeons, shamelessly relieving themselves on the stone worthies protruding from their niches along the rue de Rivoli, and on the tourists emerging goggle-eyed from the Louvre.

It was all a kind of sinister joke. And the thefts from the museum – of the *Mona Lisa* before the war of 1914, of *L'Indifférent* before the war of 1939, and quite recently of a Raphael portrait, before the war of . . . who knows when? – they were all just so many brief distractions.

2 The first corpse

I ran my chap to ground just as I was about to give up looking. It was two in the morning. He was treating himself to some solitary oysters at a restaurant near the fountain in the rue des Innocents. In the left-hand corner of the inside room, away from the noise of the traffic. Out of sight, too. If I hadn't made a habit of casting an eye well inside such places I'd have missed him.

In his sober dark jacket and his floor-walker's striped trousers you might have taken him for a member of parliament waiting for a portfolio. Especially as he looked so worried. Perhaps he took his food unusually seriously. But I hadn't noticed him doing so last May. Apart from that he was still the same, with a pleasant face, merry – but not too merry – in both senses of the word, clean-shaven as a butler and with rather heavy features. His hair had only a few streaks of silver. All in all, pretty dapper.

When I went and stood by his table he looked up and recognized me, and his eyes at once began to twinkle.

'Well, if it isn't Nestor Burma! You really are some detective!'

I shrugged.

'For once I can't claim all the credit. Your wife wrote.'

'As usual . . . Took her time, didn't she?'

'The post was on strike.'

'Oh yes . . . Well, sit down. We're old friends now, aren't we? Isn't this the third time we've met?'

'That's right.'

I hung up my hat and coat and took a seat.

'Will you have something?' he asked.

'Yes, please,' I said. 'We had a good routine going – might as well keep it up. You have let one old habit slip, though. You didn't phone me this time.'

I smiled. He smiled back.

'What does it matter? You've found me anyway!'

He held out the menu.

'What's it to be? Oysters, onion soup, or a steak?'

'I'll have the steak.'

'That makes two of us,' said Lheureux, turning to the waiter, who'd been shifting from one flat foot to the other as he waited for our order.

The waiter disappeared. Lheureux settled down on his chair and devoted his attention to me again.

'You seem to take your job very seriously,' he remarked.

'Just as well,' I said. Then, after a pause: 'Looks as if your wife's beginning to get fed up with your flying the coop.'

He waved his hand disdainfully.

'So long as she's only beginning.'

The steaks showed up and we tucked in.

'It could end badly,' I said.

He took his time chewing and swallowing a mouthful.

'No,' he said. 'I know Emilie . . . Anyhow, I'll soon be going home. Tomorrow. The day after tomorrow at the latest. Unless the railways go on strike now . . . Shall we talk about something else?'

We talked about something else and went on eating. As we did so I looked at Lheureux. Yes, I thought, he certainly is a funny sort of bloke, and Mme Lheureux must be a funny sort of blokess. And their marriage a funny sort of marriage, and Nestor Burma a funny sort of detective to let customers like this pay for his tobacco, among other things. Customers who're not worried about getting value for money; who feed you as well as financing you. The kind, as Gaby said, that we could do with more of.

It all began in 1952.

One fine May morning I got a letter, posted in Limoges, from a Mme Emilie Lheureux. She said she'd seen my name in the paper and found my address in the phone book. She apologized for bothering me on such a small matter, and one so far outside my usual scope, but if I could find it in my heart . . . She was sure I'd soon put things right. In short, her husband had done a bunk. He was probably in Paris. She didn't mind him having a bit of enjoyment – life in the provinces isn't much fun, and in the spring a middle-aged man's fancy . . . (Mme Lheureux was very understanding, and must have been extremely fond of her husband.) But she didn't want the joke to go on too long. It was a question of dignity. Her dignity. So if I could find her husband and put him on the train back to Limoges . . . She supplied a few details that proved of not much help, but enclosed a photograph of the fugitive that was eventually useful, and a money order that came in handy straight away.

I found my man quite quickly thanks to a colleague of my friend Superintendent Florimond Faroux, whose job was keeping a check on hotels. Once the truant had been located I managed to make his acquaintance and get on

quite friendly terms with him. One day when he'd had a
few and his resistance was low, I took the opportunity of
reading him the riot act and advising him to go home. (And
he old enough to be my father!) This touching scene took
place in a suitably traditional setting – the *Père Tranquille*
restaurant near Les Halles, the central food market. As
I'd now revealed my profession and the mission entrusted
to me, Lheureux merely laughed. A detective, eh? What a
scream! Emilie must have been reading too many thrillers.
But he behaved more sensibly than I'd expected, and I
soon received another letter from Mme Lheureux; a letter
of thanks.

The months went by, and May 1953 came round. I'd
completely forgotten my temperate voluptuary (his spree
had been on the most modest scale), when he rang up and
announced that he was back.

'Hallo? Is that Nestor Burma? . . . I'm on the razzle
again! Hasn't my wife let you know?'

'Not yet.'

'It won't be long! Meanwhile, to simplify matters,
why don't you come and pick me up at my hotel? It's
the same one as last year . . . That's right, in the rue de
Valois. We'll paint the town red if you're not too busy on
other jobs. And we'll settle what train I take home.'

I'd thought he was rather a wag the year before,
but now I could have sworn he was taking the rise out
of me.

'We'll see who has the last laugh,' I said to Hélène, my
secretary. 'But as he's inviting me to share his excesses I
shan't wait to be asked twice.'

And I picked him up at his hotel that evening.

In the meantime I got Mme Lheureux's letter. It
was much the same as the one the previous year, but

seemed slightly more tense. The joke was wearing thin. But although I thought I detected a faint tremor of anger in her handwriting, her instructions were the same: get the absconding husband off on the train as fast as possible.

And I did so a few days later, after accompanying Lheureux on all his nocturnal jaunts. He'd already got set in his ways. (He knew Paris quite well already from having lived there for some years in the past.) But his idea of a night out was terribly provincial, and his timetable as regular as clockwork. Restaurants, theatres, cinemas, sacrifices to Venus – everything was done at a fixed time and in the same place. Even with the same companion. And he was always perfectly correct, even when drunk. Except for one time when he sent a female tramp packing. But tramps, male and female, cling like leeches – they've no idea how to beg discreetly.

Anyhow, in a nutshell, it all went off the same as in 1952, and I put old Lheureux on the train to Limoges one night when he'd had a skinful. And as there's a divinity that looks after drunks, he got home safe and sound.

Everyone was pleased: Mme Lheureux, who received her husband back quickly and in good order; her husband, who'd got used to my keeping an eye on him; and yours truly, who'd been paid to make M. and Mme Lheureux as happy by nature as they were by name. I only hoped the same thing would happen every spring.

But it was only January now. Louis Lheureux had brought spring forward, thumbing his nose at the calendar, whether Gregorian, Russian or natural. (In my opinion a Lheureux calendar would be an improvement on them all.) And if I was to believe Madame's letter – the usual one, but this time showing definite signs of anxiety and impatience, and delayed because of the strike – he'd already been in Paris for several days. It was clear Mme Lheureux would soon be dispensing with my services. I could feel it. And I had to admit I hadn't been much use to her. The farcical situation whereby I was paid by the wife to find the husband, and entertained by the husband to keep him company, couldn't go on for ever. Perhaps it was because I had a presentiment that I wouldn't be looking after him much longer that, although he hadn't called to tell me he was here, I'd set out at once to find him. Maybe I was hoping for one last good treat.

Good treat!
Who'd be a detective!
After ordering a dessert, Lheureux got up and went to the gents', leaving me alone with a portion of Brie. As I ate I looked through a copy of the previous day's paper that had been left on a nearby chair. M. René Coty, second President of the Fourth Republic, had addressed the customary New Year message to both chambers of parliament. Emile Buisson, public enemy No. 1, was on trial with all his gang. There was a housing crisis in Berlin, where the four great powers couldn't agree on where to meet. The search for the little Raphael painting stolen from the Louvre was proving fruitless. In London, Scotland Yard's latest mystery took the form of the barefoot body of a thriller writer found in the street. And in Morocco –

I suddenly looked at my watch. It had stopped. I dislocated my neck craning at the clock in the other room, then threw the paper aside. As I thought. Lheureux had been away an unconscionable time. He'd given me the slip – there's no holding some of these hicks. I tried to see the funny side, but didn't succeed. I called the waiter and asked for the bill.

'You're not waiting for that gentleman, are you?' he said, nodding his ill-shaven chin at Lheureux's empty chair.

'I'm not in the mood for any more jokes,' I growled.

He couldn't have seduced an actress from the Comédie-Française with the tip I left him.

It didn't make things any better that it was drizzling outside, though if I felt irritable as I wove my way through the heaps of smelly vegetables it wasn't because of the local colour. Lheureux had made a fool of me, there was no getting away from it. He was more sociable in the spring. Apparently he prefered to keep me out of his escapades at this time of year.

But after I'd gone a little way I began to calm down and take an interest in the comings and goings of the retailers, haggling as they stocked up for their shops. They don't allow their customers that privilege. Then suddenly the passers-by, the handcarts, the tattered figures drawing them, the bicycles clearing swathes through the crowd with their ear-splitting bells – all jumped hastily out of the way as a police van hurtled past.

'What's up then, Jules?' a big red-faced man in a sheepskin jacket asked a colleague, from his perch on an orange-box. 'A Renault from the Prefecture went through not long ago. Is it a raid?'

'No – just a check-up,' I said.

Behind the look he gave me lay all the steaks he'd put away during rationing. Especially on meatless days.

'Don't tempt providence,' he said. Then he gave a loud guffaw. He knew how to handle check-ups.

A skinny chap in a leather jacket came over.

'It's in the rue Pierre-Lescot,' he said.

'What is?' asked the one with the red face.

'I don't know. The place is swarming with cops.'

The big man pulled a face and said he was going for a Beaujolais.

I made my way to the rue Pierre-Lescot, which was crammed with tradespeople. A crowd had gathered outside one building, between a greengrocer's shop and a depot for ripening bananas, and was being kept under control by uniformed policemen. The van and a navy-blue Renault convertible were parked a little way off. I went towards the crowd.

'Move along now,' the policemen kept saying.

But no one took any notice. Two men who looked like inspectors were standing at the door of the building. A third soon emerged from the dark passageway and joined them. He was wearing a light-coloured raincoat, a very unbecoming brown hat and a pair of greying moustaches. It was my friend Commissaire Florimond Faroux, a superintendent in the Paris CID. I called out to him and waved. He waved back and had the cordon of cops let me through.

'What are you up to round here?' he asked, after we'd shaken hands and he'd briefly introduced me to his subordinates.

'Having a night on the town,' I told him.

'Really?'

'And I've just been diddled. Can I lodge a complaint?'

'I'm not in the mood for jokes.'

Another one. He yawned.

'I was just having a snooze,' he said. 'I was on duty, but I was having a little snooze when . . . Oh well . . . Was it you who phoned?'

'Where?'

21

'My office.'

'No, it wasn't me. What makes you think—?'

'I don't know. The fact that you've turned up here, perhaps. Does the name Etienne Larpent mean anything to you?'

'No. Why?'

'Nothing.'

He chewed his moustache for a while, then with a toss of his head that temporarily endangered his hat, growled: 'Come with me. Have you ever seen a ripening room before?'

'No, but it should be fascinating, especially with you for a guide.'

I followed him into the building, followed in turn by another cop. At the end of the hallway, under the stairs leading to the upper floors, a low door opened on to a steep spiral staircase with worn stone steps. As we went down them the air grew warmer. We came to a landing glaringly lit by the light from a little room leading off it. Inside, the floor was littered with waste paper and shavings, and a swarthy man stood checking some figures at a rickety desk while two other men with stubbly chins heaved enormous bunches of bananas about.

'*Salud*,' said Faroux. 'My friend here would like to see the rooms.'

'OK,' said one of the men, with a Spanish accent.

It all struck me as rather comic, but nobody laughed. The man himself looked very lugubrious. He signed to us to follow him, led the way into a narrow passage, switched on a light, and opened a door into a sort of cubbyhole kept at tropical heat by four little naked gas jets set along the wall. Huge hands of bananas, impaled on long iron hooks suspended from rails, were slowly turning from bright green to canary yellow.

'Very interesting,' I said. 'So what?'

'Come with me,' said Faroux.

We went back to the spiral stairs, watched by the silent banana men.

'Spanishers,' Faroux explained. 'They're quiet enough now, but usually they make a deafening racket – you'd think they were rehearsing *Carmen*. That's why they didn't see or hear anything.'

'Was there something to hear?'

'Come and see what there is to see.'

After missing our footing a few times on the slippery stairs we came to the lower basement. A latticed door, its rudimentary lock forced, stood open on to a long cellar. A dim light, from a single bulb on the landing and another hanging from the ceiling, left murky corners, probably crawling with tarantulas. Heaps of broken crates, bits of wood and all kinds of packing material were lying about, and wherever you went you trod on shavings and scraps of paper. Just as you did upstairs, and everywhere else in this God-forsaken neighbourhood.

Two shadows stood out against the wall at the far end of the cellar. The shadows belonged to a couple of cops, and were cast by an acetylene lamp held by a third. They were all looking down at something on the ground. As we came in they straightened up and drew away.

The man was wearing fine leather shoes and a dark grey, expensively tailored suit. His waistcoat was undone and his shirt unbuttoned. Despite all this he still gave an impression of elegance; he must have been pretty imposing when he was standing up. But now he was lying down, and due to remain so. One or two bullets had blown away half his face.

3 Collision course

'Oh, here you are, boss,' said one of the cops nervously, flexing his knees to relieve his little stiff legs. 'We thought we'd take his clothes off, but—'

Then he noticed me, and stopped.

'Later, later,' said Faroux with a lofty wave of the hand. Then, turning to me: 'This is it,' he said, pointing to the body stretched out on the earthen floor.

He looked at me as I looked at it. Only the corpse wasn't looking at anybody or anything.

'You never know what you'll find in Les Halles,' I said. 'What was the name you said?'

'Larpent. Etienne Larpent. Does it remind you of anything now?'

'No . . .'

It was true the name meant nothing to me. But the remaining half of the face was remarkably like the face of Lheureux. If it hadn't been for the different suit . . . But was it really possible he could have left me in the lurch in the restaurant, changed into these smart new clothes, and come to show them off in a cellar to the sound of pistol shots?

'I was just wondering, though,' I said, 'how you come to know his name.'

'I'm not sure of anything yet,' said Faroux. 'There are some visiting cards with that name on in his pocket, but it may not be his suit. There's no money on him whatever. Someone must have stolen a pretty fat wallet – he obviously wasn't hard up. As you may have noticed, he didn't buy his clothes off the peg. And he may have been staying at the Transocean Hotel in the rue de Castiglione – there's one of its cards among the others in his pocket. We phoned them and they said they've got someone of that name registered there. But he hasn't been identified yet.'

'I see. What do you want me to say? "Thanks very much for the show, Florimond – I can think of more amusing entertainments, but thanks all the same"? But I can't help wondering why I was invited. May I go now? Because—'

I pointed skywards like the Statue of Liberty.

'Because the spics up there are practically sure they didn't see me lurking on the stairs or anywhere else in the neighbourhood, aren't they? So I suppose I'm free to leave?'

'Oh, so you noticed?' he laughed, not in the least embarrassed.

'What do you think? You can't catch an old monkey like me with a bunch of bananas. But why do you always assume I'm mixed up in your cases?'

'Not always,' he said. 'Only when you happen to be hanging around where the trouble starts. Then I take it as a sure sign.'

'Well, this time you're wrong.'

'Perhaps. But I can't afford to leave any stone unturned. I don't know anything about this chap yet, except that his name may have been Etienne Larpent and he may have been staying at the Transocean. But I have a feeling this is no ordinary affair. He might easily have lain here till midday before anyone noticed him. Instead of which, he's hardly snuffed it – he'd scarcely been dead for an hour – than someone rings up my office to say a man's just been killed in the cellar of a certain house in the rue Pierre-Lescot. The caller sounded quite genuine, they told me, so we took his story seriously and came round right away. I thought our caller might be someone who'd found the body but didn't want to get involved; who wanted to do his duty, but preferred to avoid bother. It's a point of view. But when I saw you up there among the rubbernecks I imagined the mystery man might be you.'

'Well, he's not.'

'On the face of it, it wasn't impossible. You could have been working on a case, this death could have some remote connection with it, and while you couldn't tell all, you still didn't want to conceal a murder. Something like that.'

'I'm not working on any case, and it wasn't me who phoned. Sorry to disappoint you.'

'Never mind. There *is* another hypothesis.'

'And what might that be?'

'That it's the murderer himself who rang up. He kills his victim, choosing a place where he can operate undisturbed and no one's likely to come for several hours. Then, having done the deed, he decides for some reason or other to inform the police. It sounds crazy, I admit. And if that's the explanation, and the caller wasn't just a respectable citizen too timid to do more than his bare duty, well, I've got a complicated case on my hands.'

'It's all yours,' I grinned. 'I'm so altruistic I'm going straight home to bed. Have fun!'

When I surfaced in the street again it was still drizzling,

though that didn't slow down the traffic. I wasn't going home to bed. *I* had some checking up to do too. Until I got to the rue Coquillière the street was crowded, mostly with night-workers, shopkeepers and down-and-outs; not many revellers. The people had thinned out by the time I got to the rue du Bouloi. Cars and vans belonging to suburban tradesmen who'd driven in to the market were parked all along both sides of the street. They were of all shapes and sizes and every age and make. I noticed one van with its right-hand door missing, but no one was likely to steal it. There wasn't a soul to be seen in the rue du Colonel-Driant; the rue de Valois was deserted. The Bank of France lowered over everything; there didn't seem to be anyone on duty there. Wet pavements gleamed like dark mirrors under the lights. Peace, perfect peace. Quiet as—

My reverie was disrupted by the screech of a car skidding in the Place du Palais-Royal, just by the Magasins du Louvre. Then the purr of the engine faded away in the darkness.

Lheureux's hotel was not far from the house where, according to the plaque, Robert Houdini had his theatre. The two lamps by the entrance had been extinguished long ago, but a ray of light from the hall reached as far as the middle of the street.

Inside the hotel the receptionist sat dozing at the desk over a sporting paper. The sound of the doorbell woke him as I came in. He started, straightened up, and gave me a drowsy smile. I'd seen him earlier the same evening, when I'd come to make sure Lheureux was staying at his usual modest hostelry. And he knew me before, from Lheureux's previous visits.

'Good evening, monsieur,' he said. 'M. Lheureux is back.'

He wasn't dead, then.

'Well . . . er . . . ' I stammered, smiling nervously. 'It's a bit late, but perhaps . . . if he's not been back long and hasn't gone to bed yet . . . ?'

'He won't be in bed. He's leaving. He asked me to get his bill ready.'

The receptionist had some sort of family connection with the place, so the owners gave him quite a lot of responsibility.

'I'll ask if he can see you,' he went on, careful not to show any expression.

'I'd be very grateful,' said I.

To hell with my reputation. And Lheureux's.

'Do you remember my name?'

'Yes, monsieur – Nestor Burma. The detective.'

I slipped him five hundred francs. If you must you must.

'Don't go imagining things,' I told him.

He pocketed the note.

'We never imagine anything in the hotel trade,' he said. 'We haven't got time.'

'Put the money on "Will o' the Wisp",' I said.

'Thanks for the tip,' he replied.

He picked up the internal phone, exchanged a few words with the invisible party at the other end, and hung up.

'Monsieur Lheureux is expecting you,' he said.

He told me the room number and left me to find my own way, which I had to do through dim corridors that still seemed to think there was a war on.

Lheureux was dressed in exactly the same clothes as he'd been wearing when he gave me the slip in the restaurant. Plus a hat. A small case lay open on the bed; he really did seem to be getting ready to leave. A bottle of whisky and a half-full glass, together with a railway timetable, stood reflected in the mirror over the mantelpiece. There was a smell of cigars.

'Making tracks?' said I. 'Going home?'

'Looks like it,' he answered. His voice was slightly blurred.

'Emilie will be pleased.'

'Yeah.'

He stuffed some more clothes in the case.

'A nice trick you played on me just now,' I said.

He grinned.

'Never mind. I'll add it to your wife's bill.'

'Do that!'

He grinned again. I yawned.

'Right,' I said. 'Goodbye, Lheureux. I'm supposed to pack you off home, so I won't delay your departure.'

'Goodbye,' he said, turning to refill his glass. He didn't offer me a drink.

I went back downstairs, my pipe clenched tight between my teeth, which didn't do my headache much good. I didn't feel tired, but I did have a headache. Once outside I hared along as fast as I could, nearly coming a cropper once or twice on the greasy pavement, till I got to the van I'd noticed earlier – the one that had a door missing and wasn't likely to attract thieves. How wrong can you be! According to the words painted on the side it belonged to 'L.B., fruit and vegetables, Châtillon-sous-Bagneux, Seine.' He was unwittingly going to do me a favour. The street was still deserted except for the parked cars. I got behind the wheel of the van and started to extricate it. Despite its dilapidated appearance it was in excellent mechanical condition and started straight away. No one shouted 'Stop, thief!' after me. I made for the rue de

Valois, muttering the Lord's Prayer backwards under my breath, and stopped, with the engine still running and the bonnet pointing towards the Place du Palais-Royal, a little way away from the hotel. Almost at once I saw Lheureux come out carrying his case, his head bowed against the rain. A few seconds more and I'd have missed him.

I spurred my old jalopy forward. The creaks and groans of its ancient coachwork made Lheureux look round. There wasn't time for him to get out of the way. I hauled on the steering-wheel. The headlights threw his enormous shadow on the dark damp wall.

'My God,' I breathed. 'Don't kill him!'

It was a near thing. Through the knobbly seat sticking into my rear as if it were full of peach stones – shades of the 'fruit and vegetables' – I could feel the van skidding over the slippery road and on to the pavement, where it bowled Lheureux over like a ninepin. He crashed down on the wing of the van and his case flew open over the bonnet, strewing his things in all directions. I reversed as smartly as if he'd pushed me. He lay in the gutter, groaning for all he was worth. I speeded away, narrowly missing a convertible at the corner of the Place de Valois, then made my escape from that place of ill omen with the verve of a Grand Prix driver.

I left the van outside the Central Income Tax Office in the rue du Louvre, hoping it would incommode one of the inspectors. Then I dived back among the grub-merchants and went and swallowed a few restoratives at a bar in the rue Pirouette.

When I felt more my usual self I waited a bit longer, then used the phone in the bar to call the hotel in the rue de Valois. This time the receptionist was wide awake.

'It's me again – Nestor Burma,' I said apologetically.

'I'd like to speak to Monsieur Lheureux, if he's still there.'

'He's in hospital!' the young man said. 'Some guests are nothing but trouble!'

I pretended to be surprised.

'In hospital? What on earth—?'

'A car banged right into him just as he was going out of here. A drunken driver, I expect. I don't know – at night only one car goes past every three hours, and I'd be surprised if there were two drunken drivers a year! And M. Lheureux has to choose just that moment! You'd think these oafs from the sticks did it on purpose!'

'Was it serious?'

'It could have been worse. The van might have gone right through our front wall! By some miracle it didn't, thank goodness.'

'I meant was M. Lheureux seriously hurt?'

'Oh, him! That was a lucky escape too. He did look a bit the worse for wear, but I don't think it was fatal. At least, I hope not.'

I hoped not too. And with a little more fervour than young Amphitryon.

'You were saying, about the hospital . . . '

'I called the police in the rue des Bons-Enfants. They came and took him away . . . ' He was getting rather testy now. He'd had enough of this affair. 'I presume they didn't put him in the clink.'

'You never know with them,' I said. 'Well, goodnight!'

I went from the bar to the police station in the rue des Bons-Enfants. They've always been a bit suspicious there since Emile Henry blew the place to kingdom come, causing half a dozen of the 'good children' in question to win a posthumous medal from the Prefect of Police.

But what the hell – I took the risk. I wasn't carrying a mysterious parcel. I had no problem getting in: I gave my own name, mentioned that Superintendent Florimond Faroux was a friend of mine, and said I knew Louis Lheureux and had just heard about his accident. And so on. The 'good children' reassured me. Lheureux had been injured in the leg, but his life didn't seem to be in danger. For further information I should apply to the Hôtel-Dieu. Just for the look of the thing I encouraged the cops to try to find the driver responsible for the accident, then left.

I felt too tired to go all the way home. The agency was only a stone's throw away, in the rue des Petits-Champs, and there was a divan there. So I went and called the Hôtel-Dieu from the office. I managed to get news about the patient without too much difficulty. There was no cause for anxiety. He'd be up and about in a few days. I thanked them and hung up. Then undressed, collapsed into bed, and fell fast asleep.

4 Diverse reports

It was my secretary, laughing, who woke me up when she came on duty at nine o'clock next morning.

'Hallo, boss,' she said. 'Having a nice lie-in?'

'Hallo,' I yawned. 'Don't I get a kiss?'

She smiled.

'I never kiss drunks. And I suppose one may assume from the fact that you're here that you were in no condition to go home last night?'

'You ought to work for a detective,' I said.

'In other words, you tracked down your Lheureux?'

'Would you mind opening the shutters?'

She let in a shaft of grimy, gloomy daylight.

'Foggy, I presume?'

'Yes, but not cold.'

She closed the windows and came over to take a look at me.

'H'm. What a face! I can see you went on a binge together.'

'Of course. My face always insists on following me about.'

'I meant Lheureux. Has he been leading you astray again?'

I laughed.

'I hope you put him safely on his train afterwards, anyway,' she said.

'As a matter of fact I didn't. He's in hospital!'

Hélène's beautiful eyes opened wide with astonishment.

'And his wife pays you good money to look after him! What happened? Did he get into a fight? Did a porter in the market try to throttle him?'

'No, just a stupid accident. Apparently a drunken driver ran into him. I wasn't there . . . Come to think of it, I ought to let his wife know. Will you send a wire? Something reassuring. And put in a personal phone call too – I'd like to put her fears at rest myself. Make it plain in the telegram there's no need for her to come. She's not required in Paris, for the moment.'

'He's not dead, is he?' said Hélène with a frown.

'Of course not! What an idea! Go and make us a pint of coffee while I get dressed.'

She vanished into the tiny kitchen, and soon reappeared bearing two steaming cups.

As she sipped she pursued her previous train of thought.

'I'm not suggesting you kill people,' she said, 'but you must admit corpses seem to crop up in your vicinity. Very odd.'

'You ought to grow a moustache,' I replied, putting my cup down. 'You talk like Faroux already – people wouldn't be able to tell you apart if you had whiskers . . . He was saying much the same thing earlier on.'

'You see? Tell me about this corpse, boss. Was it put there specially for you?'

'What corpse?'

She shrugged.

'They found a murdered man in Les Halles. Didn't you know?'

'Yes.'

'You see? I forget what his name was.'

'Larpent. Etienne Larpent. Now do *you* see? I know everything.'

'They say he's the one who stole the Raphael from the Louvre.'

'Oh? Now there's something I *didn't* know. Is it in the papers?'

'No – it was too late to get into the morning editions. I heard it on the radio.'

I went over and switched on. The voice of Catherine Sauvage singing 'L'Ile Saint-Louis' wafted into the room. I turned the volume down.

'What else did they say?'

'I wasn't paying much attention. But I think that was all.'

'We'll wait, then. I dare say Marc Covet will ramble on about it in the midday edition of the *Crépuscule*. Would you phone that wire to Mme Lheureux now, please?'

She went through into the office, and I followed her to look through the mail. There was a letter from Roger Zavatter, one of my agents already on a job.

'*I'm writing to you on our client's paper,*' it said. '*Classy, eh?*'

It was fine quality paper, with a watermark depicting a yacht surmounted by the initials P.C. In the top left-hand corner there was an engraving of the same vessel, surrounded by its name spelled out in scarlet letters: *The Red Flower of Tahiti.*

'*This is to tell you there's still nothing to tell you, except perhaps that our client's barmy. Nothing serious, though. Anyhow, no enemies on the horizon either to port or to starboard, and I wouldn't mind being his bodyguard for the rest of my life. We'll be in Paris by the 13th or 14th . . .*'

I looked at the calendar. Today was the thirteenth.

'*We'll be mooring in the yachting harbour – that is, in Paris itself. I'll let you know when we get there. A kiss to Hélène. Best wishes to you. Roger.*'

'He's got a funny way of writing a report,' I said.

'What's new?' asked Hélène.

'Nothing, really. They get here today or tomorrow. And Roger sends you a kiss. That's all.'

She sighed.

'We don't need any soap around here. All this kissing. Hasn't he got anything better to do, looking after M. Corbigny?'

'Being a bodyguard isn't all that engrossing.'

I put the letter away in a drawer and filled my pipe.

'What does M. Corbigny want a bodyguard for, anyway? What's he afraid of?'

'Zavatter hasn't managed to find out yet. And when we were first setting up the job, by correspondence, Corbigny didn't say and we didn't ask. Don't you remember? – the money order he sent was enough. Do you want to know what I think? I reckon Corbigny's a rich old eccentric – Zavatter says he's barmy, but he's a bit intolerant – a rich old eccentric, then, who owns a couple of châteaux in the Rouennais and usually travels about by boat, and like a lot of people with too much money, he's bored. So instead of hiring an ordinary companion he invents imaginary enemies and treats himself to a private detective with a gun. It adds a certain spice to his existence.'

'And it doesn't do ours any harm!'

At this point one-armed Reboul, the third of Nestor's team, breezed in.

'Don't waste time sitting down,' I said as he made to pull up a chair. 'You've got an errand to do at the Hôtel-Dieu. You know I'm supposed to be guarding the virtue of one Louis Lheureux—'

'The chap who turns up regularly every year?'

'Yes. His virtue's intact, but I believe his legs are no better than they should be. He had an accident, and they took him to the Hôtel-Dieu. I want you to keep an eye on him. If he has any visitors, try to find out who they are. Use your own discretion.'

'OK,' said Reboul, without asking for any more explanations.

He left. Hélène looked at me, amused. Just then the waiting room bell went and the door opened.

'Hi, folks!' said Superintendent Faroux.

'What, another body, sheriff?' I growled.

'I don't know,' he said. 'I'll have to look under the furniture . . . Am I allowed to sit down?'

'By all means. But what brings you here? Last night's body? I thought I said I didn't know him from Adam.'

He sat down.

'And I believe you.'

'One swallow doesn't make a summer,' said Hélène.

Faroux wagged a finger at her.

'Don't come running to me to give you a kiss next Christmas,' he said.

'She's more likely to run if you try,' I said. 'She seems to have some sort of phobia. And now, enough of the lady-killing. I can tell you've got an ulterior motive.'

'All right.' He cast a look round the office. 'Very busy?' he asked.

'So-so.'

'Right. As I was saying, I believe you. So much so that I'm going to ask you to do a little job for me. A confidential job. The official police can't take care of everything. Sometimes they haven't got much room for manoeuvre. They can be very glad to have a private eye handy—'

'To take care of certain delicate operations?'

'Exactly . . . Well?'

'I don't like the sound of it. Your lot seem to think that because you use informers you might as well go the whole hog and hire a private eye – is that it?'

He scowled. 'I wouldn't have put it like that.'

'The way it's put is neither here nor there. You're not a bad sort, but you're a cop . . . What's it worth?'

'Being a cop?'

'The job, the job.'

'I haven't got a budget for it myself, but I'm sure you'll manage to fiddle something out of it somehow . . . Just take a look at these.'

He took a couple of photographs from his raincoat pocket and passed them over.

'I always knew you'd end up flogging postcards,' I said. 'I see you're getting your hand in . . . And who might this little vamp be?'

'How does she strike you?'

'I wouldn't mind spending some of my spare time with her.'

'Only some of it?'

The photos showed an elegant young woman in a dress

with a neck so low it nearly came down to her ankles. What you could see of her was pretty good, and what you couldn't see must have been even better. She had a delicate oval face with a fine nose, sensuous lips, and languorous eyes behind long lashes. Shell-like ears are too common in this connection to be worth dwelling on, but for the record she had shell-like ears with pearls nestling in their tender lobes. Her hair was drawn severely back, but instead of making her look like a schoolmarm this only added a piquant dash of reserve to the overall oomph.

I passed one of the photographs to Hélène for her to get an eyeful, even though it wasn't quite her style.

'Do you know her telephone number?' I asked Faroux.

'Telephone number, room number, name – the lot,' he answered jovially.

'And what do you want me to do?'

'Go to bed with her!' he laughed.

'Hélène,' I said, 'the tape-recorder's on, isn't it? . . . Good. You see what the police are finally reduced to? Pimping. I didn't want to believe it, but there it is. Now we've got proof.'

'No, but seriously,' said Faroux. 'You can sleep with her if you like – and if you can. It can be your fee. Do you know who she is?'

'You tell me.'

'Her name's Geneviève Levasseur. Her friends call her Jany or Jenny – something like that. She works as a model at Roldy's in the Place Vendôme – you have to pass the time somehow – but she doesn't have to live off her salary. She used to be Roldy's mistress. Then she moved on to a jeweller in the rue de la Paix. And there's an ex-minister somewhere or other in the background. She's dabbled in films, too. All in all she's very well known and influential – a woman of the world, you might say. But there's a snag in all this, and one *we* can't exploit to the full because of her connections. The snag is, she was recently the mistress of . . . Larpent . . . Etienne Larpent.'

'The chap who was left to ripen in Les Halles last night?'

'That's right.'

'And whose real name wasn't Larpent, if I'm not mistaken?'

Faroux raised his bushy eyebrows. 'What makes you think that?'

'You hesitated when you said it.'

'OK. No, he isn't really Larpent. The real Larpent has got a record. He was sent down for two years for fraud in 1925. He hasn't been heard of since, but that doesn't mean anything. He was called Marius Daumas in those days, but we called him Will o' the Wisp because he was always popping up where you least expected him. When I say he was called Daumas – that was the name he used, but it isn't a common name in the north of France, is it?'

'Was he from the north?'

'Yes. From a place that suffered badly in the 1914 war. Shelled to smithereens and all the records destroyed.'

'Very convenient.'

'Yes.'

'And the Will o' the Wisp went on living off ill-gotten gains, did he? They say on the radio he was the one who nicked the Raphael.'

Faroux waved dismissively,

'Completely phoney,' he said.

'What! You put out false news on the wireless now, do you?'

'I don't mean the news. I mean the picture.'

'For a servant of the state you haven't got a very high opinion of its museums.'

'I'm talking about the picture we found on the body. We thought at first it *was* the Raphael, but the experts say it's only a rather poor fake.'

' "Found on the body"? . . . Oh yes, I see.'

The papers had said the stolen picture measured about eighteen inches by nine – quite easy to hide once it was removed from its frame. I recalled the scene last night in the rue Pierre-Lescot.

'He was carrying it next to his skin, and your chaps had just opened his shirt and found it when you and I arrived – is that it?'

'No flies on you, eh?'

'You said it. I'm not a civil servant with a monthly salary – if I don't keep my eye on the ball I don't eat.'

'You're going to have plenty to keep your eye on now.'

He picked up one of the photos and ran a grubby finger over Geneviève's delightful face.

'Her, you mean?'

'Yes. Not that she's a suspect. It's not a crime to sleep with a crook who's managed to lie low for nearly thirty years – even if he does get himself bumped off with a copy of a stolen picture on him. If the false Larpent was engaged in any dirty work, she doesn't seem to have known about it. Larpent – let's call him that for the moment – didn't live in Paris. Like all the filthy rich, he only came up to town from time to time. According to the register at the Transocean in the rue de Castiglione – we'll check up on it – he booked in there a week ago, coming from Switzerland.

'I said Geneviève Levasseur was his mistress, but that's

a bit misleading. She only slept with him occasionally – this year, and last year, on a previous trip of his to Paris. She didn't travel around with him. For two years she's hardly stirred from the Transocean, where she's a permanent resident. As I said, we've got nothing against her. We don't think she killed this bloke. There's always the possibility of a crime of passion, of course, but her alibi is sufficiently vague to be convincing. And she hasn't tried to hide her relationship with him – she admitted it of her own accord when we were checking up last night at the hotel. The pair of them seem to have been so discreet I doubt if we'd have noticed anything if she hadn't told us about it herself. Mind you, when she found out what had happened to her lover, and our low opinion of him, she seemed sorry she'd spoken. But by then it was too late.

'So, we've nothing actually against her, but because she was mixed up with Larpent we can't help being interested. I can't have her watched too obviously because she'd notice and object. And with all her influential friends—. Although she identified the body, we shan't mention her name. We'll just say it was someone who knew him. And it's better if we don't go tramping around her in our great big hobnailed boots. Whereas . . . '

'Whereas an elegant gent like me . . . '

'Precisely.'

'Spare me the soft soap. I do wear my clothes well, as they say, and certainly no one would ever take me for a cop. But I'm not a real gent. If I were, I'd turn down your suggestion and show you the door.'

'And if I were a real cop I wouldn't put up with your cracks for five minutes.'

'Right. Now we've got all that straightened out, let's have the dope.'

'You know her name's Geneviève Levasseur. You know she lives at the Transocean Hotel. The room number's 512 – the top floor, but nothing like an attic.'

'Are the beds comfortable?'

'I'm not sending you there to sleep.'

'Who said anything about sleeping? . . . And she works for Roldy, the couturier?'

'Yes – she's a model.'

'OK. What do you want me to do?'

'Worm your way into her confidence.'

'How?'

'I thought Nestor Burma was irresistible.'

'Not always. Still, I'll try. How old is she?'

'Thirty – but she only looks twenty-five.'

'So she must be thirty-five.'

'No. Thirty.'

'All right. Even if she *was* thirty-five I wouldn't say no. So I'll try to worm my way into her confidence, as you put it.'

'Not too unpleasant a task, wouldn't you say?'

'Tasks palmed off on other people are always pleasant.'

'Anyhow, keep your eyes skinned, and if you come across anything interesting—'

'My dear Faroux,' I said, picking up one of the photographs, 'if I do come across anything interesting and it's a question of choosing between your moustache and this pair of—'

'You'll go for the reward,' he interrupted.

I looked at him.

'Oh, we're serious now, are we? What *is* the reward?'

'Three million francs.'

'Offered by the Friends of Immortal Masterpieces, I presume?'

'Something like that.'

'Pull the other one. The Friends are a sham, and the reward is a sham, just like the picture Larpent was using for a vest.'

'Not exactly.'

'Oh yes. It's all a ploy to set the art thieves at loggerheads, so that one of them will blow the gaff in order to get the reward. But the silly fool won't get a penny. Am I right?'

'Not exactly,' he said again. 'There will be a reward, if someone respectable finds the painting or points the way to it.'

'So I'm in the running?'

'I'd say you'd got a fifty per cent chance,' he laughed.

'A fifty per cent chance of three million francs is not to be sneezed at.'

'So how much is the picture itself worth?' asked Hélène.

'A few hundred million.'

'Good gracious!'

'Exactly!'

'Anyhow, it's worth the effort of trying to find it,' said I. 'But tell me – was Larpent the one who stole it or not?'

'We don't know,' said Faroux with a sigh. 'We're just groping in the dark. We've got several theories. First – ' He held up a nicotine-stained finger – 'First, he really was the thief. He had both the genuine picture and the copy on him, and someone relieved him both of his money and of the original. In which case the criminals must have been his accomplices. Unfortunately, in the present state of our knowledge, we don't know where to look for them.'

'And, if they exist, they'll have skipped.'

'Yes. And anyhow the few people he's known to have seen since he arrived in Paris are all beyond reproach. The second hypothesis,' he said, aiming two fingers at my pipe, as if challenging the bull on it to a fight, 'is that he had only the forgery, which he'd had made for some nefarious purpose. Such as giving it back to the museum as if it were the original – apparently something of the sort happened over the *Mona Lisa* in 1912. Or perhaps he meant to palm it off as genuine on a collector. In any case, he was killed by someone who was only after his money.

'We prefer the first of these two theories, but there is quite a plausible variation on the second. Larpent might have belonged to a gang trying to exploit the theft of the Raphael, and some row might have broken out between them in the cellars under the rue Pierre-Lescot.'

'But why there?' asked Hélène.

'The cellars and passages under the streets of Paris don't change much,' said Faroux. 'Especially in Les Halles. As I told you, Daumas, alias Larpent, was in trouble with the law before. Well, the chap he swindled all those years ago had premises in Les Halles, and Larpent must have been familiar with all the nooks and crannies. He must have come and reconnoitred, then arranged to meet his crony or cronies there. *He* may have wanted to pull a fast one, but the others were too quick for him.'

'And made off leaving the picture wrapped round his corpse?' I said.

'Well, that's where we found it.'

'Why would they do that?'

'Perhaps the deal they meant to do with the copy hadn't worked out, and the money in Larpent's wallet would cover their expenses – apparently he always carried a lot of cash around. Or there could be other reasons.'

'Because they were interrupted, you mean? Or because it was dangerous to hang about?'

Faroux shook his head. 'They weren't disturbed, and they could have stuck around as long as they liked. They could have played a game of poker if they'd wanted to.'

'Maybe they started one, in a way . . . And apart from all that – any clues?'

'Not a thing. But I'm keeping an eye on a couple of painters in Montparnasse who've attracted attention before because of their skill at copying. And on two or three unscrupulous collectors. We're also making inquiries about the respectable people Larpent happened to have dealings with – but I know that won't produce anything. There's nothing against Mlle Levasseur, either, but I'm proceeding on the principle that she's the weak link. If anything gives – if! – it'll be there. But as I've explained, unfortunately *we* can't tackle her openly. So—'

'She'll be in good hands,' said Hélène.

'I'll do my best,' said I.

'I hope so,' sighed Faroux. 'You won't be needing the photographs?'

'I'll manage with the original.'

He put the two pictures of Mlle Levasseur away in his breast pocket.

'But I don't promise anything *will* give,' I said.

'Except the lady's bra straps,' said Hélène.

5 Floating thoughts

There were three of them sitting in the foyer in overstuffed chairs and killing time. Another crime that doesn't pay. If they'd had to struggle for their crust they'd have put a bit more vim into it. One of them was admiring his feet, another couldn't find anything of interest in the paper, and the third was scowling disapprovingly at the rococo ceiling. Admittedly it was dated, but if it clashed with the present it did so politely. Mustn't give offence to the Transocean's well-heeled guests.

The concierge preened himself behind a desk as shiny as a good tip. He was cool, stiff, smooth and grave – very conscious of his own importance. It lends a person status, being flanked on the left by one of the most famous squares in Paris, if also the dreariest, and on the right by the Tuileries Gardens, so quiet and peaceful and cosy – when there's not a wind of revolution blowing. But talking of revolution and the Place Vendôme: perhaps, as an employee, however superior, he was dreaming of the pikes brandished by Sade and other eminent forebears. These flunkeys are so stately and impassive you can never tell what they're thinking.

He looked me up and down, but couldn't detect anything objectionable about my silk scarf, natty trilby, tweed overcoat and elegant suit, worn just casually enough to show I wasn't dressed up. I'd put away my pipe so as not to offend anyone's sensibilities, and was newly shaved, with no unsightly gashes. Got up like this I could easily pass for a prosperous member of one of the liberal professions, or someone in films. Nothing remotely like a cop, private or otherwise.

Since Faroux's visit to my office I'd managed to think up an excuse for approaching Mlle Levasseur, and now proposed to put it to the test. But the lady herself and the blue-uniformed concierge combined to save me the trouble.

The former was out, and the latter couldn't tell me when she'd be in. I could leave a message if I wished. I didn't wish. I said I'd try again, and blew.

Mme Lheureux would soon be calling me back on the phone, so I set out to walk back to my office. But at the corner of the rue de la Paix and the rue Danielle-Casanova I felt a presence behind me. Turning round unobtrusively, I noticed among the other passersby a man who looked too unconcerned to be so. He was very well dressed, with a swarthy complexion and a thin moustache; his hands were in his pockets; he was smoking what looked like an expensive cigarette. That was all I could see from where I stood. But we used the same crossing to get to the other side of the avenue de l'Opéra, and we were close enough then for me to examine him further. He had a long face, with a big chin and grey eyes that seemed quite uninterested in me. When we'd crossed the street he started to walk more slowly, but still in the same direction.

I ought to set up as a guide, I thought. My favourite beats seemed to appeal to visitors.

By the time I got to the Passage Choiseul he'd reached the corner of the rue Ventadour. I dived into the building where the Fiat Lux Agency has its headquarters and rushed up the stairs three at a time. Once in my office I flung open the window and looked out into the street. No one. At least, not my chap.

'What's wrong?' said Hélène. 'Feeling faint?'

'I've got off with a dirty young man,' I told her. 'It's this area. He must have taken me for a midinette. He followed me here, and I wouldn't be surprised if he's coming up the stairs right now . . . '

He wasn't, though. When I looked out again I saw him crossing over and standing thoughtfully on the pavement in the rue Sainte-Anne. I shut the window.

'My turn now to follow him,' I said.

But just at that moment the phone rang.

'It's for you,' said Hélène. 'Limoges.'

I took the receiver.

'Hallo, Limoges! Burma here.'

'Good afternoon, monsieur,' said a young female voice obviously more used to calling the cattle home.

'Good afternoon, Mme Lheureux.'

'Oh, I'm not Mme Lheureux. I'm Mariette, the daily help. Mme Lheureux can't come to the phone. She's an invalid.'

'I see. Very good,' I said.

'Don't be so heartless,' said Hélène, who was listening on the earpiece.

'I mean . . . er . . . I didn't know,' I said into the phone.

'Everyone here knows, monsieur.'

'Of course, of course. Well, listen, Mademoiselle Mariette: M. Lheureux has had an accident . . . '

I made her learn by heart what to say to Mme Lheureux – nothing to worry about, et cetera – sent my best wishes, et cetera, and rang off.

When I went back to the window my pursuer had vanished.

'Well, we won't let it take our appetite away,' I said to Hélène. 'It's past lunch-time, and I've got a good idea where to look for our friend. If I'm not mistaken I first noticed him ensconced in a club armchair in the foyer of the Transocean.'

We looked through the early evening editions of the papers as we ate. The headlines were full of Larpent's murder and the discovery on his body of the Raphael copy. There was a photograph of the painting too; it didn't say whether it was of the true one or the sham. No photo of the dead man, though. Admittedly he hadn't been a very artistic sight when I saw him in the cellar. And apparently they hadn't found a presentable picture of himself in his effects. Anyhow, what purpose would it have served? Despite the headlines and all the space accorded to the incident, the papers were extremely reticent. There was no reference to Larpent's past, except that he'd come to Paris from Switzerland and had been staying in a fashionable hotel. They didn't give the name of the hotel. Nor was there any mention of Mlle Levasseur. As Faroux had said, the body of the dead man had been indentified by 'acquaintances'.

Back in the office, by way of dessert, I called the publicity-sensitive Transocean. My hunger remained unassuaged. Mlle Levasseur was still out.

Soon afterwards the phone rang. Roger Zavatter, the freshwater salt.

'Hallo, boss. We've berthed.'

'Where are you phoning from?'

'A bar by the river.'

'I thought you weren't supposed to let Corbigny out of your sight?'

'He's crazy!' he exploded. 'To think it's always blokes like him who are rolling in money! To listen to him you'd think everything in the world was insufferably boring. He can't stand it! . . . His nerves, you know . . . And I believe he's thinking of dispensing with our services – I shan't have lived the life of Riley for long. You'd better come and put the wind up him – invent some danger or other.'

'You'd like to go on being his bodyguard, then?'

'I should think so!' he laughed. 'No rough stuff, good pay. It's a cinch. If only we can make it last.'

'Well, as Corbigny's a client I suppose I really ought to set eyes on him once. I'll come. Where are you?'

'The Port du Louvre.'

'And the boat's the *Red Flower of Tahiti*?'

'No. That flower has faded. Trouble with the engine. But Corbigny's loaded. He's got another yacht. We're on the *Sunflower* now.'

'A great botanist, eh?'

'No, lettuce is what interests him,' said Zavatter. 'It'd be a pity to let him slip through our fingers.'

The smart little yacht was bobbing gently on the yellow waters of the Seine between the Pont du Carrousel and the Passerelle des Arts. With its sails furled, if that's the right term, and its mast down, it looked like an ordinary boat, only rather cleaner. A member of the crew, got up like a caricature in a thick blue jersey, canvas trousers and a peaked cap, was standing on the deck watching a string of barges go by down the middle of the river. Hearing me step on to the landing plank, he turned and came to meet me. His cap was adorned with the traditional red anchor; all that was needed to complete the picture was a wisp or two of fog. But the midday sun had dispersed the mist that had hung over Paris in the early hours.

'Hallo, admiral,' I said. 'I'm Nestor Burma. The name should mean something to your boss – "captain", perhaps I should say.'

'Boss'll do,' answered the circumnavigator of the Canal de Sceaux. He looked more likely to spread his bait in the Boulevard de Sebastopol than on the banks of Newfoundland. 'He's no more a captain than I'm an admiral.'

'Only joking,' I said.

'Huh . . . And what makes you think—'

'It's my chief, Gus,' interrupted Roger Zavatter, emerging from the cabin. 'You can let him through.'

He led the way into a luxurious cabin, furnished with taste and originality and with an eye to comfort too. A neat little old man with white hair, a sallow skin and sharp teeth that matched his nose, sat moodily smoking a cigar.

'This is Monsieur Nestor Burma,' said the bodyguard.

The elderly eccentric got nimbly to his feet, smiling faintly, and shook my hand. His own was wizened but wiry.

'How do you do, Monsieur Corbigny?' I said.

I signed to Zavatter to go on deck and watch the barges go by.

'You're a client of the Fiat Lux Agency,' I went on. 'We've dealt with each other by correspondence so far, but as the opportunity to meet you presented itself . . . I like to meet my clients in the flesh. I hope I'm not disturbing you?'

'Nothing disturbs me!' he growled. Then: 'Sorry – please forgive me. I'm a bit nervous.'

'Aren't we all?' said I. 'It's these modern times. But surely life afloat is more peaceful?'

'No – just the same! All the boats have got engines now.'

Could he be hankering after the epic days of sail?

'Anyhow . . . Would you like a drink? I'm on a diet myself, but . . . Do sit down.'

I installed myself on a plush-upholstered bench. The floor moved up and down underfoot. I don't much care for that sensation when I haven't had anything to drink. I could hear the water slapping the sides of the boat and washing against the stones of the quay, together with the sound of motor horns and the murmur of traffic.

What with all this and the weariness that still persisted from my exploits of the night before, I felt as if I were wafting about in a dream.

But Pierre Corbigny had a strong sense of reality. At present, at least. He opened a sliding panel in the bulkhead, revealing a shelf of books and a range of bottles capable of satisfying the most demanding toper. He selected a vintage brandy and poured me a glass.

'Very good,' I said when I'd tried it. 'And is my man?'

'I beg your pardon?'

'Is the bodyguard I supplied giving satisfaction?'

'Yes indeed. A very cheerful chap.'

'But he can be very useful too if the occasion arises. Though I don't think it has, has it?'

'Not yet.'

'I'm not sure if I should hope it does or not!'

He didn't bite.

'I don't know either . . . A little more brandy?'

After refilling my glass he contemplated the bottle for a moment, then went and fetched a glass for himself.

'In your honour,' he said, 'I'm going to forget about my diet. A little drop shouldn't do any harm. If I do snuff it, the name of the killer's on the bottle.'

He swigged it down and coughed. The second glass went down more easily.

'So is his job at an end?' I asked.

'M. Zavatter's, you mean?'

'Yes.'

'Not at all! What could have made you think that?'

'Nothing. I just wanted to be sure he suited you, and that you wanted us to go on looking after you.'

'But of course.'

'Excellent!'

At this point the chap with the anchor on his cap came into the cabin for some kind of orders, then swaggered off again with what he took to be a nautical gait.

Corbigny shrugged and gave a quiet laugh.

'Have you ever thought, M.Burma,' he said bitterly, 'what a sham some people's lives are?'

Fortunately he didn't wait for an answer.

'Did you see that?' he asked.

'What?'

His eyes darkened.

'That idiot of a so-called sailor! It's grotesque! I don't feel in the least like laughing, but sometimes it's difficult not to. I don't know why it is, but sometimes, like today, certain things strike me as more than usually ridiculous. That fool of a Gustave pretends to be a sailor – and the sight of a packet of salt is enough to make him seasick!'

'I'd noticed something of the sort,' I said.

'You see! Oh well, who am I to make fun of him?'

He warmed to his task.

'A day-dreaming old dotard! Wishing I'd been a pirate in the West Indies, or sailed round Cape Horn. I was born a couple of centuries too late . . . But what rot!' he blurted out angrily. 'The most difficult thing I ever navigate is the Pont-Neuf, and my only buccaneering consists in cheating on my income tax. That is, as much as a respectable education will let me. Everything's a sham, I tell you. This is the age of trash and substitutes.

'It seems that even in there' – he jerked a thumb at the Louvre, which could be seen through the porthole – 'even in there, if we're to believe the papers' – this time he pointed at a copy of *Le Crépuscule* lying on the table – 'they hang up forgeries for all the visiting imbeciles to swoon over. Don't you think that's funny?'

'No,' I said, laughing, 'because what you say isn't true itself! You're referring to the copy of the Raphael that's mentioned in the papers, I presume?'

'Yes.'

'They don't say it was exhibited instead of the original.'

'Who's to say? I know what I'm talking about. I've got my own theory.'

I pricked up my ears.

'I've had it since 1912 . . . '

I let my ears fall again. I wasn't concerned with ancient history.

'Yes, monsieur. Ever since the *Mona Lisa* was stolen and then put back again, no one knows if it's really the genuine article. That's historical fact! And although you must have been very young at the time, you'll have heard how Marcel Duchamp drew a moustache on it at the beginning of the Dada movement, and how a great poet, another famous pioneer, got into trouble over it . . . '

'Apollinaire,' I put in, trying to cut the lecture short.

But it was no good, and when, after a long disquisition about Apollinaire's life and death, I made my escape, I understood why Zavatter thought M. Corbigny was touched.

Apart from anything else, Zavatter wasn't very well up in poetry. He once took Mallarmé for the nickname of a crook whose gun didn't go off.

Back on dry land, I went into a bar and phoned the Hôtel-Dieu for news of Louis Lheureux. They said he was getting on all right, and I set out for my office, making a detour via the hotel in the rue de Valois.

The receptionist I'd seen before – Albert, his name was – had just come on duty. His pink cheeks bore witness to a day spent in the open air, and he was poring, pencil in hand, over a couple of racing papers.

He didn't seem terribly pleased to see me. Like a good many other people, he associated me with trouble. Still, even if he couldn't forget how Lheureux had been skittled outside and nearly got the hotel frontage bashed in as well, he might have remembered that I'd slipped him five hundred francs.

'Good evening, monsieur,' he said without enthusiasm.

'I was just passing and I thought I'd call in to let you know how your guest was.'

'M. Lheureux? How is he, then?'

It was plain he didn't give a damn.

'He'll survive.'

'Oh, good.' He gathered up his papers.

'What was the going like today?' I inquired.

'All right for the nags. *I* lost a packet,' he growled.

'Too bad . . . Oh, by the way,' I said as if the thought had just occurred to me, 'what happened about Lheureux's luggage?'

'Luggage? He only had one little case.'

'What became of it?'

'Hasn't he got it with him?'

'Apparently not.'

He gave me a sidelong glance, hesitated for a moment, then said with a shrug: 'You'll have to ask the cops about it. They picked him up, bag and baggage. His things were all scattered about – it was only a trashy little case and it burst open.'

' "We live in an age of trash",' I said.

'Eh? . . . Anyhow, I stuffed all the things back as best I could, and the police took it away with them. I suppose they must still have it, unless they've chucked it away. Don't ask me.'

'Thanks. And better luck tomorrow.'

He didn't answer. I saw his reflection in the glass as I went out through the door. He was scowling after me and scratching his chin. Obviously a few hours' sleep wouldn't do him any harm, and the healthy air of the racecourse had stimulated his beard and made him itch like mad.

6 Beware of Greeks

A big surprise was waiting for me at the office.

For who did I find sitting in the chair provided for clients, a pair of hogskin gloves resting on his hat, his hat resting on his knees, and his eyes resting on the agreeable profile of Hélène Chatelain as she pounded on her typewriter?

The chap who'd followed me that morning.

He stood up and bowed ceremoniously.

'Good evening, M. Burma,' he said.

His voice wasn't unpleasant: rather singsong, with a slight and undefinable accent on certain syllables.

'I think we've met before, Monsieur . . . Monsieur . . . ?'

Hélène stopped typing and consulted a scrap of paper.

'Monsieur Kirikos,' she said.

'Bi,' said the visitor, smiling politely. 'Birikos. Nicolas Birikos.'

'Same thing,' said Hélène. It was clear she didn't like the look of his frizzy hair, heavy chin and thin lips.

'As you like,' said the Greek. Someone must have told him it wasn't chivalrous to contradict a Frenchwoman.

'As I was saying, M. Birikos,' I resumed, 'we've met before.'

'Very possibly.'

'You were watching flies in the foyer of the Transocean this morning.'

'Yes, that's where I'm staying. But there aren't any flies in Paris at this time of year.'

'It was a figure of speech.'

'Well!' exclaimed Hélène. She'd realized who he was, and was looking but not saying 'Of all the cheek!'

'And having watched the flies,' I went on, 'you proceeded to do what the flies do to the fly-paper.'

He smiled, and bowed again. He had a very supple back.

'You mean I stuck to you.'

'Precisely.'

'I won't say I came just to apologize for following you, monsieur, but . . .'

'Well, what can I do for you?'

He hesitated.

'Perhaps after all I'd better just apologize and go. There's no reason why you should satisfy my curiosity.'

'Just a moment,' said I. 'Apart from anything else, I'd very much like to know why you *did* follow me.'

He looked round the room.

'Do you think we might sit down?' he said.

I led the way into my office and offered him a chair. He sat down, offered me a Turkish cigarette, took one himself, and lit both with what looked like a solid gold lighter. When all these formalities were completed he sat back and began.

'Paris is an astonishing city . . .'

Nothing to disagree with there. Even if it did sound

as if he was embarking on a speech to the mayor and corporation.

'Some of the things that happen here are quite . . . how shall I put it . . . ?'

'Astonishing?'

'Yes . . . I was trying not to repeat myself . . . Anyhow, I was sitting in the foyer of the Transocean this morning, bored as usual . . . Though something did happen yesterday . . . Something that didn't suit the hotel, perhaps, but what's that to me? Anyway, we found out that one of the guests, M. Etienne Larpent, whom I knew by sight from having passed him in the corridor and the lift . . . Well, they said this M. Larpent . . . '

'Had been murdered?'

'Yes. Extraordinary, wasn't it?'

'Seems pretty commonplace to me.'

'To you, perhaps. But you're a detective . . . We afterwards learned that M. Larpent was . . . how do you say . . . ?'

'In trouble with the law?'

'Yes. I found that fascinating.'

'And?'

'Er . . . '

He seemed at a loss.

'Am I boring you?' he asked.

'Not at all. Go on.'

He drummed on the brim of his hat. His fingers were rather fat, and didn't go with his long thin face.

'Yes, I am. I'm boring you,' he said. 'So I'll be as brief as I can.'

That wasn't saying much.

'I found myself taking an interest in M. Larpent,' he said. 'I get very bored, you see . . . So, I was sitting in the foyer when I overheard you asking if Mlle Levasseur was in. Now I know that Mlle Levasseur'—He smiled. The smile of a voyeur. '—was Larpent's mistress. So I was interested, and – I don't know why – I followed you. And when I found you were a private detective I was overjoyed. It was all so mysterious! But afterwards I saw I'd behaved incorrectly, and that it was my duty to explain myself in case you'd noticed and started to imagine things. After all, in your profession . . . So please accept my sincere apologies.'

He made as if to leave.

'Just a moment.'

'Yes?'

'You say you were curious. Perhaps I can satisfy your curiosity.'

'I wouldn't like to take advantage . . . '

'What is it you wanted to know?'

'Well, I thought that as you knew Larpent . . . '

'I didn't know him,' I said.

'You didn't!'

'No.'

'You astound me. I seem to remember Larpent mentioning your name one day. I can't be absolutely sure, but it *is* a rather unusual name . . . Still, if you say . . . '

I said nothing.

'So I thought that as you knew Larpent . . . But of course, if you didn't, that alters everything.'

'Assume for the sake of argument that I did.'

His eyes lit up again.

'I thought you might be able to tell me some things about him that don't appear in the papers.'

'What for?'

'Just by way of distraction. I know it sounds silly.'

'I can't tell you anything,' I said.

'I know I'm ridiculously impulsive. First I follow you, and then I ask you to reveal professional secrets.'

'It's not that,' I said. 'I can't tell you anything about Larpent because I don't know anything. And I don't know anything because I didn't know *him*. In my opinion, if anyone knew him it was you.'

He hesitated.

'Well, yes. I admit I knew him slightly.'

'Have you told the police?'

'No. I don't think it would have helped them, would it? And I really don't wish it to be public knowledge that I have been even slightly connected, merely out of politeness, with someone who it seems was some kind of gangster. I'm a respectable citizen, monsieur. Foolishly romantic perhaps, but respectable. Here—'

He fumbled in his wallet, got out a card, and put the wallet away again.

'Here's my card. I run a very successful business in Athens, and scandal can damage a business, even from hundreds of miles away. I haven't told the police I knew Larpent, and I don't propose to tell them. If you see fit to do so I shall deny it, and they won't be able to prove otherwise. But I hope you won't tell them.'

'I won't,' I said. 'There's no reason why I should. But as you're so romantic and eager for distraction, I'll provide you with a little.'

I picked up the phone and dialled the Transocean.

'I'd like to speak to M. Nicolas Birikos, please.'

'He's not in, monsieur.'

'But he is one of your guests?'

'Yes.'

I asked a few devious questions designed to find out

if their Birikos was the same as the one sitting in my office.

'Excuse my checking up on you,' I said, putting down the phone.

'Of course.'

'At least you make no attempt at concealment,' I remarked.

'Why should I?' he said, putting on an innocent expression. 'I'm just a foolish, harmless romantic. I made a wrong move with you. I apologize again, but . . . '

He rose.

'You have my name and address. If ever—'

I stood up too.

'By the way,' I said, 'you're not a collector, by any chance, are you?'

'No. Do I look like one?'

'I don't know. Perhaps we'll meet again, M. Birikos.'

'I hope so.'

I saw him to my door, then Hélène took over and saw him to the top of the stairs. Back in my office I noticed a scrap of paper under the chair he'd been sitting on. It must have dropped out of his wallet. As I picked it up the doorbell rang again. I stuffed the piece of paper in my pocket and nearly bumped into M. Birikos as I turned round.

'Excuse me,' he said. 'Did I leave my gloves?'

He looked round in exasperation. I looked round too. Not a glove to be seen.

'Oh!' he exclaimed, 'they're in my pocket! I must have put them there without noticing – I was so embarrassed!'

He brandished them and put them on – like that he wouldn't lose them again. He took leave of us once more with his usual ceremony and left, this time for good.

I went over to the window, opened it and looked out.

M. Birikos was standing on the pavement, gloveless again, oblivious of the people swirling round him, and hunting anxiously, very anxiously, through his pockets. He got his wallet out of his overcoat and checked it, put it away again and went through his pockets once more. Finally he moved gloomily away.

'What is it?' said Hélène. 'Has he lost his gloves again?'

'No. This bit of paper.'

It was only a torn-off scrap of ordinary paper. It had the word 'Mégisserie' written on it.

'It must be part of an address – "Quai de la Mégisserie", no doubt. Foreigners often write the names of places down as reminders, even if they know Paris quite well. He seemed very bothered about it, didn't he?'

'Yes,' she said. 'Though he didn't look a very likely visitor to Mme Stambat's salon.'*

She's very well up in Paris high life, my secretary.

'Who knows? Do *I* look like a picture thief?'

'We-e-ll . . . '

'OK – lend me a thousand francs and I'll bet you our Greek pal takes me for Larpent's accomplice.'

'No! That's all your reputation needed!'

'Anyhow, I've got a job for you. I want you to keep an eye on a racegoer. His name's Albert and he works in the Hôtel des Provinces in the rue de Valois. He lives there too, and never goes anywhere else except to the races. Get yourself up to look as if butter wouldn't melt in your mouth, take a room in the hotel, and watch him. There's something funny about the way he goes on, and I want you to find out what it is.'

* It was in the Quai de la Mégisserie that the late Mme Sophie Stambat used to hold one of the last of Paris's literary salons.

'Isn't the rue de Valois where Louis Lheureux hangs out every year?'

'Yes.'

'Hmm . . . '

She didn't say any more. Just opened a cupboard and got out the sort of case a respectable young lady would travel with.

'And he was supposed to be such an easy customer. No trouble at all!'

'No trouble!' I sighed . . .

The rue des Petits-Champs became as quiet as the grave for a while. Then the phone rang.

'Yes?'

'It's Hélène.'

'OK?'

'Yes.'

I hung up. It was lucky there was a room free in the rue de Valois. I started to think about Albert. Funny kind of chap . . . Again the phone interrupted my meditations.

'Reboul here.'

'What's new?'

'Nothing. No visitors. Condition satisfactory. Should be allowed out in a few days' time.'

'So it wasn't serious.'

'More frightened than hurt.'

'Good.'

'He sent a letter to his wife.'

'Like a dutiful husband.'

'He could have got out of it. He had to get another patient to write it.'

'Something wrong with his arm?'

'I suppose so . . . Shall I stick around tonight? I've worked it so that I can come and go as I like in the hospital.'

'That'll come in useful when we get shot.'

'Hadn't thought of that. So what am I to do?'

'Use your own discretion, as usual.'

I hung up, then dialled another number.

'Transocean Hotel,' said the voice of a stuffy type in a stiff collar.

'Mlle Levasseur, please.'

'Mlle Levasseur is out. Would you care to leave a message?'

'No, thank you. Is M. Nicolas Birikos there? I don't want to speak to him – I just want to know if he's there.'

'No. M. Birikos is out.'

I rang off, tucked the visiting card and the scrap of paper in the corner of my blotter, and stood up. Then I gave my pipe a good clean, filled it, lit it, put on my coat, and went out to see if the cold dark night held anything in store for me.

It did. The usual. A nice bang on the head.

7 *La vie Parisienne*

The cobblestones were sticking into me, and my bruised
hands scrabbled at them, heaven knows why. What did
I want with cobblestones? I wasn't going to build a
barricade. You build barricades in the summer. Step
up and see how people die for twenty-five francs a day.
How much was I dying for? Three million – a nice round
sum; if I got it. If I got it, it would pay my doctor's bill.
The cobbles were wet and slippery, and I was slithering.
I'd have given a lot – not the three million though – to be
able to stand up. But I couldn't.

So I crawled.

I'd had a terrific thump on the head. Or rather two.
Probably three. Same number as the millions.

I crawled.

The cobbles were sharp, wet and cold. I could hear
water flowing not far away. Softly. Treacherously. Making
a very sinister sound. Everything was dark. There were
some lights twinkling away in the distance on a massive
shape, even darker than the darkness, that looked like a
bridge. But all around me, darkness.

I crawled on.

The water was flowing louder, nearer now, unless my

ears were playing tricks on me. A horribly smelly object came and settled not far from my cheek.

'Don't go no further, pal,' said a boozy, guttural voice.

My numb fingers closed on the smelly object. It was a foot. It had a leg attached, and so on. The voice came from on top.

'You trying to chuck yerself in the river?'

'Dunno,' was all I could manage.

'Crossed in love, eh?'

'Dunno.'

'I'd better get you under cover. Don't forget, I'm saving yer life. Don't forget, eh? If it hadn't been for Bébert you'd have been in the juice.'

He bent over me, his breath nearly turning my stomach in the process, then got hold of me under the armpits, hauled me along a little way, and deposited me under a bridge.

'A visitor for you, Duchess,' I heard him say. 'From high society! Fell out of his car. Or was chucked out.'

'I was hit on the head,' I mumbled.

'Could have been hit *and* chucked,' said the tramp. 'Anyhow, I saw the car, and I saw you fall out of it.'

'Assault and battery,' croaked a woman's voice, ageless and almost sexless. 'He'll mean trouble.'

'No, no!' I croaked back. Trouble was Nestor Burma's special privilege. I wasn't going to share it with anyone else.

'He's my pal,' said the man. 'I saved his life. He won't forget. He'll give me a reward.'

I felt him going through my pockets. I offered no objection. It wasn't the first time I'd been searched that night. It was in fact the third, if my poor aching bonce hadn't given up on me altogether.

(It had started in the bird shop, though I didn't know at the time that that was where I was.

It had been a very bad idea of mine, going for a stroll along the quai de la Mégisserie. That's where I'd received the first thump on the head; I'd have been better off going to a café. There weren't many people on the quai, but there was one too many: the bloke who knocked me out just by the rue Bertin-Poirée. (I could remember the place – that was something.) When I came to a little while (or perhaps it was a long while) later, I was still wondering how it had happened. I hadn't anything better to do, of course. And it had seemed to me then, although I was still comatose, that someone had gone through my pockets.)

'What are you up to, Bébert?' asked the female tramp.

'P'raps he's got an address on him – someone to be notified in case of accident.'

'Come off it, Bébert. You can't read. Leave him alone.'

I stretched. It was nice to be able to, even if it hurt; even if I was still lying under a bridge, sheltered from the rain but not from the wind.

(It came back to me that the first time I'd recovered consciousness I'd been tied hand and foot, and it was as difficult to work free as to get a month's grace from my income tax inspector. I didn't even try. (I do try with the income tax man.) I was in a very strange place. Dark, and full of strange stirrings and rustlings. It was cold, and smelled of something like bran or corn. For some reason or other I tried to whistle, and it was then I realized I was gagged as well as bound. And my eyes must be blindfolded. I rolled over, and as I did so I knocked against something and set up a deafening racket and a great flapping of wings. Then a canary gave an angry trill, a ringdove cooed. I was in a bird shop. And I'd been snared and caged like all the rest.)

'Get him back on his feet with a drop of wine,' said the female tramp.

'He's my pal,' said the man. He struck a match.

(I'd woken all the birds, but the din they made didn't bring anyone running. It was much later on that some one came. I couldn't see him because of the blindfold, but I could tell he was nervous and anxious. He too went through my pockets, then stood me up, and . . . And nothing. That was my second bang on the head.

The next time I woke up I was on the river bank, no longer bound and gagged, dragging myself dangerously near the water but stopped just in time by a tramp who claimed I'd been tossed out of a car. But I must have been dreaming. It didn't make sense, all that. I'd been attacked, hit on the head, tied up, left all alone with the birds, then put back in circulation. But what was the point? I hadn't been asked any questions. I *must* have been dreaming. And I must be dreaming still. What was it all in aid of? Unless they'd stolen my wallet. But then why all the complications? . . .)

A draught had blown out the man's first match. He'd struck a second, and now there was a persistent yellow flame – they must have lit a candle. And as through a mist I saw the male tramp handing my wallet to his equally tattered companion.

'You look through it, Duchess – you can read.'

A short silence.

'He's a cop,' said the woman. 'I told you he was trouble.'

'Cop or not, he's my pal. I saved him, and he'll remember. If he's a cop he'll give us a hand somehow . . . '

'He's not a real cop. He's a private detective.'

'Is he a cop or isn't he?'

'Sort of.'

'Hell! Give us his loot quick and I'll put it back.'

'I know this man,' said the Duchess in an altered voice. 'Him and his brother.'

The man leaned over me, holding my wallet.

'We haven't pinched anything, pal. We're not thieves. But don't forget what I did for yer, will yer?'

He slipped the notecase back in my pocket. The light went out. I heard bottles clinking, then a gurgle of liquid being poured and the smacking of lips.

'Hi, Duchess,' the man protested, 'you haven't started drinking alone, have you?'

'I need warming up,' said the woman, throwing in an oath for good measure.

'Hand it over.'

'No, I'll give him a swig myself.'

I heard her coming over.

'Light up, Albert,' she said, 'so I can have a look at his mug.'

'OK, Duchess.'

Another match was struck.

'Drink this,' she said. 'It's lousy stuff, but I can't afford anything better. In the old days I used to have a good cellar.'

I feebly pushed the bottle away. I don't usually turn my nose up at a drop of wine, but at that moment I couldn't face it.

'It's not wine,' she said, as if she could read my thoughts.

'Not wine?' the man mumbled, dropping the match in his surprise. 'What is it then?'

'Rum.'

'Oh, been hiding things from me, have yer?'

'Yes, I have.'

'Let's see the label.'

'There isn't one. And put the blasted light out – someone'll see it . . . Have a good swig, love.'

This last was addressed to me.

I had a pull at the rum. It did me good.

'Feel better?'

'Yes.'

'That'll be a hundred francs.'

'All right.'

'You can pay when you go.'

'All right.'

'Do I get some too?' said the man.

'You can have the rotgut. Here . . . '

He drank and coughed.

'Lovely stuff,' he said.

'Lousy,' said the old girl.

I could feel a coat or something being spread over my legs. I lay where I was. It wasn't as cold as I'd have expected under the bridge, or else it was the rum taking effect. I could feel my strength slowly coming back. As soon as I could manage it I'd rush back to the agency and rest my ill-used head on a nice clean pillow. The two tramps huddled beside me, muttering together and occasionally passing the bottle back and forth between them.

'I know this bloke,' whispered the woman. 'Or someone very like him. A chap I used to know when I was well off.'

'When you were a duchess,' sniggered the man.

'When I was Aurélienne d'Arnétal.'

'Come off it! You don't come from Darnétal – you were born in Villedieu-les-Poêles!'

'Don't be daft – I couldn't call myself that! And I couldn't call myself d'Alençon because Emilienne had already used that. She got in first. My "reign" didn't start till 1925.'

' "Reign", she calls it!'

He spat.

'That was the expression, ignoramus! . . . Anyhow, I called myself d'Arnétal, and there were these two blokes and they both wanted to sleep with me. Both at once, practically!'

'Only two? I thought you had all the upper crust.'

'Stupid! Haven't you ever heard of Aurélienne d'Arnétal?'

'Hell – since I met you I've never heard of anything else!'

'And before you met me?'

'Yes – I'd heard the name. Wasn't she a famous tart? One of the "queens" of Paris?'

'There you are, then! I used to have motorcars, servants, a mansion in the avenue du Bois and a house in the country . . . It's not all that long ago . . . 1925 . . . '

He sniggered.

'House in the country! I'll bet!'

'And why not? . . . Pass the bottle.'

'It's empty.'

'Greedy swine!'

They started squabbling, then calmed down. My head was feeling better. Not spinning round so fast. There was no point in staying there and catching pneumonia. I got to my feet. Yes, I could manage.

'Where are you going, pal?' said the tramp.

'I'm off. I've got a bed somewhere.'

'You're lucky,' said the woman.

'I'll say.'

'I used to have a bed, once.'

'With lots of mugs in it,' said the man.

She laughed but said nothing.

I took out my wallet, and got another surprise. My money hadn't been touched – I could tell by the feel of the notes. The more I thought about how I'd been attacked, the less I could see any point in it. I selected a few notes and stuffed them into the first hand I encountered in the dark.

Then I tottered off.

I tottered to the rue des Petits-Champs, and it seemed a long way. I passed a number of nightbirds, but not a single cop. Just as well. I'd no idea what the time was. My watch had stopped. All I knew was that it was still dark, and so much the better.

It took me a good quarter of an hour to get up my two flights of stairs. I was so exhausted my eyes were half closed, and behind the lids floated an enticing white mirage consisting of clean sheets and pillow cases, a bed, a marvellous soft warm mattress . . . They all awaited me beyond this door with 'Fiat Lux Agency. Director: Nestor Burma' painted on it. The door was the last obstacle between me and the bed. But I couldn't find my keys. At last I discovered them, not in the usual pocket.

I opened the door and dragged myself through the waiting room and into Hélène's office. Take my advice – don't make plans. My bed was stretching its arms out to me in the next room, but something told me it would be some time before I could fall into them. Hélène's office was in a mess. Half-open drawers had obviously been gone through. Files had been taken down from the shelves and not replaced. Slowly, just as if I were some ordinary detective, it began to dawn on me why I'd been attacked. I made my way to my own office, opened the door and switched on the light, halting on the threshold to enjoy whatever spectacle had been prepared for me. I wasn't disappointed. The scene was the same as in Hélène's room. It was difficult to say, at first blush, whether the burglars had taken anything. But it was very plain that they'd left something behind.

The elegant fawn shoe didn't look as a respectable shoe ought to look when it's empty. But it wasn't empty. There was a foot in it. One extremity of a normal human body in a fairly good state of preservation. The carpet had been rumpled, and the man was lying with his face buried in its folds. Disregarding my own weariness, I took hold of his hair, gently lifted his head, and had a look at his face. A little way on the wrong side of forty. He wouldn't be going any further. Grey eyes, thin moustache, thin lips, frizzy hair. Nick Birikos. The Greek. Not bearing any gifts.

I went on into the room with the divan, but resisted its temptation. Instead I poured myself a restorative, swallowed some aspirin, and propped myself against the wall for a while. When I felt strong enough I went back to the corpse and searched it. It seemed to be the night for going through other people's pockets. But my examination of the body produced nothing, unless you count a few bouts of nausea. No passport, anyway. There were various documents, including a driving licence, all in the name of Nicolas Birikos from Athens. Some money. Not much. Enough to pay for cleaning or even replacing the carpet, though, so I pocketed it. That was all there was for me. No clue. No indication of what the Greek had been looking for in my office, when instead he'd found death.

He'd been shot through the heart. From the disorder of the room and certain other evidence, in particular the state of his wrists, I deduced that there'd been a struggle.

Painful as my head still was, it began to function again.

At least two people – Nick Birikos and X – had been looking for something in my records. But what? They had the advantage of me: they knew and I didn't. I'd foolishly let myself be lured into a trap designed to let them get hold of my keys and then keep me out of the way.

Apparently they'd found what they were looking for, whatever the hell that might be, and then quarrelled, presumably because each of the thieves wanted from then on to go it alone. The rash Nick Birikos had pulled a gun, but had somehow fallen a victim to it in the set-to.

X then ran away in a fright – there weren't supposed to have been any fatalities – and brought me back my keys. But it wouldn't have done for me to come to in the bird shop and so be able to identify the place where I'd been kept, so he dumped me beside the river like a sack of potatoes, hoping the cold might relieve him of the responsibility of finishing me off. X wasn't an actual killer, and Birikos had died by accident.

I went into the bedroom for another reviver, then came back into the office. The body was still there, and I didn't see how to get rid of it. The best thing was to let it lie until I hit on the least inconvenient solution. I cudgelled my brains trying to think what object it could have been that had caused a burglary, a fight, and a death. Whatever it was, it had clearly gone. But search as I might, physically and mentally, I couldn't see that anything was missing, apart from the scrap of paper Birikos had lost, and his visiting card, both of which had vanished from my blotter. But they couldn't have been the cause of all that carnage. I gave up.

It was then that I noticed a feather, a yellow feather, in

the turn-up of the corpse's trousers. A canary feather. That proved Birikos had been in the bird shop. I confiscated the clue – no point in leaving too many of them for the cops who would soon be swarming all over my office. *I*'d take care of the bird man.

I went to a cupboard and took out a jemmy. It had been left behind by a locksmith who paid me a visit one memorable day, along with a bailiff and a policeman. I'd hung on to it as a trophy.

Out on the landing, all was quiet. It was a quiet house in a quiet neighbourhood, full of quiet and slightly deaf people. I got to work with the jemmy so that it would look as if my visitors had forced the door. Then I left.

Not long after, in the Place de la Madeleine, I hailed a night cab and got it to drop me near my flat. The burglars had obviously been and searched there first; but this time they hadn't left a corpse.

I tidied up a bit, then phoned a quack I knew who lived just across the street. He moaned and groaned, but came. I asked him to give me something that would make me feel more or less normal after a few hours' sleep. He obliged without asking questions and went home to bed.

I didn't need any rocking.

8 A new client

I was woken by the sound of a bell ringing.

I got out of bed. My head had stopped spinning. I really didn't feel too bad. There must have been a bump, or even two, on my head, but they were hidden by my hair. I put on my dressing gown and looked at the alarm. Ten o'clock. It wasn't that that had woken me up. And it wasn't the phone. The ringing had been at the front door. Someone had left his finger on the bell, or rammed it with a nail from his hobnailed boot. To show I wasn't in any hurry I stuck my pipe in my mouth, drew the curtains to let in some light, then went and opened up. Florimond Faroux looked tired, and walked in almost without stopping to wipe his feet on the doormat.

'I'm in charge of the case,' he said without preamble.

'What case?'

'You notice I've come on my own. I didn't want to put you at a disadvantage.'

'Well, you have. I was just dreaming about Martine Carol.'

'Leave Martine Carol out of it.'

'If I must! Come this way.'

'Phew, what a pong!'

'Medicine. I wasn't well. That's why I slept so late. A touch of flu.'

'Yes . . . And I suppose your agency's ill too?'

'What do you mean?'

'Your staff don't come in very early.'

'They're occupied elsewhere.'

'Huh! I suppose they're out looking for bodies – the Fiat Lux Agency doesn't seem to be able to function without them! Anyhow, it was the neighbours who noticed.'

'Noticed what?'

His cigarette had gone out. He lit it again.

'You've been burgled.'

'What!'

'Get dressed. We're going to have a little talk, and then you're going to come with me. We need a statement about the damage.'

He sat down.

'Is it serious?'

'Worse than you think . . . Does the name Birikos mean anything to you?'

'First does the name Larpent mean anything to me, then does the name Birikos! – what sort of question is that?'

'Answer it instead of acting the fool.'

'All right. Birikos does mean something to me. It's the name of a Greek who came to see me yesterday.'

'Where?'

'At the agency.'

'What time?'

'In the afternoon.'

'He must like it there. He came back during the night, and stayed.'

And out he came with his story, illustrated with pictures

79

by his own pet artists. He spoke evenly, without expression, and I punctuated his recital with suitable ohs and ahs.

He didn't tell me anything I didn't know already. He and the police doctor took the same view as I had about the way Birikos had died. The accidental shot had gone unheard because my office was soundproofed.

'So what does it all mean?' asked Faroux when his narrative was finished.

I shrugged.

'Come on, Burma – your turn.'

'What do you want me to tell you?'

'Everything you know about Birikos.'

'It's not much. He was hanging about in the foyer of the Transocean when I went there to start work on Geneviève Levasseur, and—'

'Just a minute! Have you made contact with her?'

'I've done all I can, but she's never in. I hope to have better luck today – if you give me the chance. I trust you're having her watched, by the way?'

'Don't you worry. We're keeping an unobtrusive eye on her. But we can't really do it thoroughly – if she suspected anything we'd only have to stop, and then it would be the devil's own job to begin again, especially if she's really done anything wrong. That's why I'd rather leave it to you. I'd like you to take over from the men who're on the job now. You can go farther than they can. And I'd like you to make it snappy, before she notices anything's up. Got me?'

'I've got you.'

'Good. So go on about Birikos.'

'He followed me to my office. That was before lunch. I spotted him, and intended to follow *him*, but I lost him. That didn't matter, though, because he came and saw me of his own accord in the afternoon.'

'What for?'

'To try to pull the wool over my eyes.'

I explained how.

'Then he left, and I haven't seen him since.'

'You will. Soon.'

'Is he still at my place?'

'More probably in the morgue by now. Did you form any opinion about him?'

'I thought he must be crazy – unless he was Larpent's accomplice. He may have known him better than he admitted. And he was staying in the same hotel.'

'As far as we can make out he hasn't got a police record. But that doesn't mean anything. Any other ideas about him?'

'He might have been one of these unscrupulous art collectors. There are more of them than people realize. And perhaps *he* took *me* for Larpent's accomplice.'

'Explain.'

'Suppose he's waiting to receive the stolen picture. He doesn't know who the thief is, or who's in charge of the negotiations. If he knows Larpent it's only because they're both staying in the same hotel – he doesn't know his part in the plot. When he hears about Larpent's death, and learns that he had a copy of the picture on him and therefore must have been more or less connected with the original, he gets interested. Not because Larpent is dead, but because the genuine picture is still missing. He knows Mlle Levasseur was Larpent's mistress, and he hears me asking after her. He sees right away that I'm not a cop, and instinctively follows me—'

'Assuming a private eye is bound to be the accomplice of an art thief,' said Faroux with a grin.

'More or less. Private detectives get mixed up in all

sorts of things. I'm told some are so perverted they take on special duties to oblige the official police.'

'Ha, ha. Go on about Birikos.'

'Hope revives in him, and he comes and tries to pump me. I disappoint him, but he still thinks I've got the painting. So as I've ignored all his hints, he decides to take drastic measures. He comes back at night to search my office.'

'Right,' said Faroux. 'And he finds the picture. This doesn't look too good for you, Burma.'

'But he *doesn't* find anything. If I'd had the painting in my possession – though I can't imagine how I could have – I'd have handed it over to you yesterday and claimed the three million reward.'

'Pull the other one. The picture's worth several hundred million. And no doubt there's a crazy collector somewhere who'd give half that for it. And half of a few hundred million is quite a lot of money.'

'But as I told you, he doesn't find anything.'

'All right. So in a fit of rage and despair,' said Faroux with heavy irony, 'he commits suicide. Or rather he tries. But the chap who's with him tries to stop him – don't forget there were signs of a struggle. But still Birikos manages to send a bullet through his own head.'

'Don't talk rubbish!'

This gave him pause. He frowned.

'If they didn't find a picture to quarrel over, what's *your* explanation of the fight and its outcome?'

'I haven't got an explanation any more than I've got the picture . . . Unless . . . '

'Yes?'

'Birikos didn't look like a crook.'

'A bit flashy, like a lot of Greeks, but that's all,'

Faroux agreed. 'As I said, he hadn't got a record, at least in France. We'll have heard from Athens in a few days' time.'

'He wouldn't have known how to force my door on his own. He must have brought a real crook with him. And this crook . . . ! Well, that beats all! Some burglars turn my place inside out, they leave a stiff as a token of their esteem, the police pester the life out of me, and I'm five thousand francs out of pocket!'

'Five thousand francs?'

'Did you search the place too?'

'Yes.'

'And did you find any money in the top drawer of Hélène's desk?'

'Not a sou. As usual.'

'A lot you know! And on Birikos?'

'Not a sou.'

'There's the reason for the fight, then – Birikos was looking for the painting, but his temporary accomplice was after my dough. Birikos was honest, in his way, so he tried to make the crook desist by threatening him with a gun, which he'd only brought with him because he had doubts about his companion. There's a fight and Birikos is killed. The crook takes the Greek's money and mine, and goes off with the gun.'

'H'mm . . . I suppose it's possible . . . Five thousand francs, you say?'

'Yes.'

'The Fiat Lux Agency has never had that amount stashed away. I'd have known if it had.'

'All right, call it three thousand. It was worth a try – it takes so long for the compensation to come through.'

'Burma! You don't mean to say you meant to improve

the occasion by cheating the insurance company?'

I looked sheepish.

If anyone ever did give me three thousand francs it would be more than that drawer had ever contained. It swelled with pride and got stuck if you tried to stow away a tenth of that amount.

'To get back to the subject,' I said, 'that's the only explanation, if you rule out the picture. And I can tell you right away, Faroux – if you go on thinking I'm involved in *that* affair, you needn't expect me to spy on the lovely Geneviève Levasseur for you.'

'All right. I don't really think you had the picture. As for Mlle Levasseur, I've been thinking. She strikes me as too compromised to have to be handled with kid gloves any more . . . We'd better take over now and hope for the best with the high-ups . . . So you think, if Birikos followed you just because you were asking after her, that means he thought Mlle Levasseur and Larpent were in it together?'

'Not necessarily. But your guess is as good as mine.'

I accompanied Faroux to the agency, where the uniformed cop who'd been left on duty seemed to think it very funny that a private eye had been burgled. I made a statement about the damage, insisting that the non-existent three thousand francs were missing, and off we went to the morgue. I identified Birikos as categorically as if he were my own brother, and then I was free. I was back in my office by two o'clock, the usual time for people to come in after lunch, and called in a nearby locksmith to repair the door. While I was waiting for him I racked my brains again to think what the intruders could have been after, apart from the picture that had never been in my possession.

They certainly had found something, found something important – but I couldn't think what it was. Finally I gave it up, left the locksmith and the concierge in charge of the office, and set off for the National Library. I'd been wanting to consult its dusty shelves since the previous day, but hadn't had time to go there. Today I had the time, but I only wasted it. I worked my way through a heap of 1925 newspapers, trying to track down the crime Larpent a.k.a. Daumas committed around then. But as I hadn't got Faroux to give me the exact date, I didn't know where to look and didn't find anything.

So I packed it in and went back to the office. Hardly had I got in than the phone started to trill merrily through the dark.

'Hallo?'

'I want to speak to M. Nestor Burma.'

It was a woman's voice. Sweet as a bird. If only your plumage is as lovely . . .

'Nestor Burma speaking, madame.'

'Mademoiselle. Mademoiselle Geneviève Levasseur.'

I was speechless.

'Hallo? Hallo?' said the voice impatiently.

'Hallo? Yes?'

'Does my name mean anything to you, M. Burma?'

Does the name Larpent mean anything to you? Does the name Birikos mean anything to you? Does the name Geneviève Levasseur . . . ? In the end I'd say something *I* meant. Something unrepeatable.

'Well . . . '

'It wouldn't be surprising. I'm often mentioned in the papers. I'm a model at Roldy's.'

'I see.'

'Just so that you know who I am.'

'I see. And what can I do for you?'

'This is the first time I've ever approached a private detective. And even if you haven't come across my name, I've often come across yours. I wanted to ask you . . . When a person's bothered by . . . undesirables . . . can you get rid of them . . . efficiently and discreetly?'

I started to laugh.

'My goodness, mademoiselle!' I said. 'You don't mean by using a gun, I hope?'

She laughed too. A very fresh and agreeable sound.

'No, nothing quite so radical!'

'You do reassure me!'

'Could you undertake the job?'

'Probably.'

'Will you come and see me, then? I live at the Transocean Hotel in the rue de Castiglione. Can you come right away?'

'I'm on my way.'

'See you shortly, then.'

I rang off, switched on the light, picked up the phone again and called Florimond Faroux.

'What's up?' he said.

'I've taken one step towards young Geneviève's bed.'

'I thought I told you to chuck it. We're taking over.'

'I can't chuck it. She's my client now. She's noticed she's been followed. She wants me to get rid of some people who've been bothering her. That can only be your people. What a joke, eh?'

I told him about my conversation with the model.

'Hmm . . . ' he growled. 'I suppose it's quite convenient in a way . . . All right – carry on, Burma. You've got carte blanche.'

9 *High life*

She was even better in the flesh than in the photos. (It's usually the other way round.) The only thing I regretted was that her cocktail dress wasn't so low cut. But it did leave room for hope. If she bent down, for example. But I could hardly throw money down on the carpet and make her pick it up. Her arms were bare. Very pretty arms. Her legs weren't bad, either, not to mention other attractive movables. Her fair hair was combed back, as in Faroux's photograph. Her almost green eyes were made up to look slanting. Her hands were slender, with immensely long, varnished nails. Except for the right forefinger. The nail on that was varnished too, but short. It must have got broken recently, perhaps in a scrap. She looked like a girl as ready to claw as to caress.

She received me in a little sitting-room adjoining her bedroom. It was warm and comfortable; the lighting was elegant, and equally flattering to people and things. She gave me a quick once-over. Then she said languorously, 'You don't look like a policeman.'

'I'm a private detective, mademoiselle.'

'Of course . . . Won't you sit down?'

She went and curled up in a wing chair. I parked my hat on a table and sat down too.

'Cigarette?'

She held out a slim cigarette case, from which she'd just extracted a long Russian or pseudo-Russian fag – two parts paper to one of tobacco. I stood up, took a cigarette, lit both of them, ogled her *décolletage* and went back to my chair.

'I'm glad you look more like a gentleman than those other horrible people,' she said. 'But I do hope I haven't disturbed you for nothing. I'm very impulsive . . . And my nerves have been under a strain these last few hours . . . '

I treated her to a brush salesman's smile. And waited.

'My name is Geneviève Levasseur,' she said.

'Quite so, mademoiselle.'

'You don't seem to have heard of me . . . '

'I'm sorry – I'm not a regular reader of *Vogue*.'

'But you do read the papers?'

'Nearly all of them.'

'So you've come across the name Etienne Larpent?'

'Larpent? Wasn't that the man who was found murdered with a copy of the stolen Raphael on him? Either a copy or the original – I don't always swallow what I read in the papers.'

'That's the man.'

She looked at me through her long lashes.

'He was my lover.'

I didn't say anything. What did she expect? Condolences or congratulations?

'And *I* didn't kill him,' she added angrily, throwing her unfinished cigarette at an ashtray. She missed.

I got up, put the fag-end where it could do no harm, and sat down.

'Has anyone accused you?'

'Yes.'

'The police?'

'They questioned me. I gave them a . . . what do you call it?'

'An alibi?'

'That's it. We didn't go out together that night, Etienne and I. He said he had some business to attend to – I don't know what. Or rather I didn't. But now . . . Anyhow, I went out with some friends, they backed me up, and the police accepted my account. But this man says an alibi can be destroyed, and so . . . '

She paused, tucked one leg underneath her and gave me a good eyeful of the other.

'What man?' I asked.

'My alibi wasn't made up, M. Burma. I want you to believe that.'

'I believe it. What man?'

'A blackmailer. An amateur blackmailer. But I can see how ridiculous it seems now.'

'Never mind. Go on. I shan't do anything unless you instruct me to.'

'It's someone I know slightly – I met him at a cocktail party. I never gave him any encouragement, but he wouldn't be put off, if you see what I mean. His name's Maurice Chassard.'

'And that's the undesirable character you want me to get rid of for you?'

'Not now. I'll get rid of him myself. I was on edge when I phoned you just now. The whole thing is ridiculous.'

'As you like,' said I.

At that moment the phone rang. She got up to go and answer it, revealing enough thigh to arouse my cannibal instincts. She stood there in a model-like pose with the phone held to her ear while her other hand stroked her hip.

As she listened she frowned. Her expression grew hard.

'No,' she said. 'I'm not in. No . . . I . . . Just a moment.'

She put her hand over the mouthpiece.

'Perhaps you haven't gone out of your way for nothing, M. Burma. It's Maurice – Maurice Chassard. I've a good mind to see him and break off with him once and for all. Your being here will help me, and may frighten him.'

'An excellent idea,' I agreed.

She gave me a sidelong look.

'Just a minute,' she said into the phone.

She covered the mouthpiece again, turned to face me and said curtly:

'I don't like your tone, M. Burma.'

'Really? I don't understand.'

'If you think . . . if you think I killed Etienne too – you'd better go.'

She stamped her foot.

'Go on – go!'

'I don't think anything of the sort,' I said quietly.

She calmed down as quickly as she'd got worked up.

'I'm sorry,' she said. 'It's my nerves . . . Send him up!' she almost shouted into the phone.

She went and sat down again, careful now not to reveal too much. Soon afterwards there was a knock at the door, and at her request I went and opened it. As I did so a confident voice greeted me:

'Good evening, you gorgeous doll!'

'You've got the wrong person,' said I.

He drew back, stammering an apology. He smelled of

drink, and had the complexion of someone who gets up late and doesn't go to bed early. Well dressed. Perhaps a shade too smart, but nothing too obvious. Young. Brown eyes, with rings round them to match. A straight, rather long nose, the tip covered with a faint network of little blue veins. A young man of means on the spree, or a fairly harmless crook operating among the socialites. Quite good looking in spite of that nose, which might have been liver, not drink. Likeable enough, all things considered. And stronger, physically, than he at first appeared . . . I say! After all, why not? He was rather like one of those modern reporters who put their feet on the table, say 'Yeah', and wear their hat over one eye because they see too many American films.

'Come in,' I said. 'We can play three-handed.'

'I don't understand—'

'Come in!' ordered Mlle Levasseur from her armchair.

He did so without more ado, went and stood in the middle of the room, and looked first at the girl and then at me.

'I'd like you to meet M. Nestor Burma,' said our hostess.

'Nestor Burma?'

He scratched the tip of his nose.

'He's a detective,' she explained.

'Right,' he said. 'I've heard of him.' Then he laughed. 'Is he supposed to find the picture?'

'What picture?'

'Don't act stupid! Your lover was a thief. He stole a painting from the Louvre. But he's dead now, and . . . '

His voice faltered, he looked around for somewhere to sit, then collapsed on to a chair and mopped his brow. Perhaps the room was too hot for him. Perhaps he'd been drinking too much. Anyhow, young Geneviève leapt out of her chair like an arrow from a bow and stood there with her eyes flashing, her bosom heaving with anger.

'You hear him, M. Burma?' she rasped. 'You hear? He's slandering me! This wretch is slandering me!'

'Don't let's get excited,' I said. 'He's not slandering you – he just says your lover was a thief. That's very probably true. He also says he's dead. That's true too.'

She looked daggers at me.

'So you're against me too?'

I shrugged.

'That'll do! . . . Now, all things considered – if you're capable of considering – do you or do you not want me to show this fellow the door?'

'Yes!' she cried. 'Throw him out of the window if you like! That would be better still – we're on the fifth floor!'

'No fear!' said I. 'I didn't come here to end up in jug. But we ought to be able to clear up the situation without too much trouble.'

I went over to Chassard and yanked him to his feet by his lapels. He stared at me as if he was frightened to death.

'I'm not going to eat you,' I told him.

Then I let him go. He shook himself, fell back a pace or two, and said, 'I'm going!'

'No, wait!'

He froze.

'Listen a minute, M. Chassard,' I said. 'How do you make a living?'

He hesitated.

'I manage,' he said.

'At least you're frank!'

'Why shouldn't I be?'

'And since you're so frank, come clean.'

'What do you mean?'

'You're both round the bend.'

'Both?'

'You and her.'

'M. Burma!' Mlle Levasseur remonstrated. She was sitting down again now.

'That's enough from you!'

I turned my attention to Chassard again.

'So you manage, do you? You sleep with ladies of a certain age – a very certain age – and then, when you feel like having it off with a young one you don't shrink from a bit of blackmail – is that it? Just to back up your sex appeal!'

'How frightful!' exclaimed Geneviève.

I turned on her.

'Now just you listen, mademoiselle!' I said. 'Or, if you're too squeamish, go to your room!'

She stamped her foot.

'No! I'll stay. This *is* my apartment!'

'As you like. But don't keep interrupting.'

I sat down beside her so I could keep her quiet if necessary.

'So let's go on, M. Chassard!' I said. 'You accuse this young lady of having killed her lover?'

'Yes.'

'This is ridiculous,' said the girl.

She felt for my hand and clutched it tight. I could feel her breast quivering against my right arm. Chassard gazed at us, his eyes full of hatred and fear.

'Why should she have killed him?' I asked.

'So as to . . . so as to get hold of the painting.'

'You're a fool, Chassard. I've wasted too much time on you already.'

Geneviève withdrew her hand from mine.

'I advise you to give up trying intimidation,' I told him. 'It won't work. Mlle Levasseur may well have loved a man who was a thief. But she didn't kill him. I won't go into detail or make any speeches – I'll just tell you this: I'm working for Mlle Levasseur, and when you bother her you bother me. So watch out. And don't go trying to flog your stories to the gutter press, or you'll live to regret it. Get me?'

He shrugged.

'All right.'

He seemed relieved. He'd probably been expecting a kick up the arse, and was glad it had been put off. Now I came to think of it he wasn't so likeable after all.

'You can go now,' I said.

'I'm a fool,' he groaned.

'That's what I've been telling you. Cheerio, Chassard.'

He slunk out. I closed the door behind him.

'There,' said I, going over to Geneviève. 'Are you pleased?'

She hadn't put herself out for Chassard, but now he was gone she arranged herself more fetchingly in her chair.

'Thank you, M. Burma,' she cooed. 'I – I didn't kill Etienne, you know.'

'Let's not talk about it.'

'You're right . . . .Now . . . How shall I put it? . . . What are we going to do about your fee?'

'You can pay me later. When it's all finally sorted out.'

'But I thought . . . '

'With a bloke like that you can never be sure. It'd be just as well if he thought I was still around for a few days . . . If you have no objections, of course.'

She gazed meditatively at her shoe. Perhaps she was thinking that no sooner did she get shot of one nuisance than another took his place.

'But of course, M. Burma,' she said at last.

'I'll try to be as inconspicuous as possible,' I told her, smiling.

She smiled back.

'In that case, Chassard won't be very scared.'

'That's not what I meant.'

'I understood what you meant. Thank you, M. Burma. And goodnight.'

She held out her hand meaningly. I kissed it. I haven't had much practice at that kind of thing, but I did my best. I didn't do badly. As I picked up my hat I brushed a yellow card on to the floor. I glanced at it almost involuntarily as I picked it up, and saw it was an invitation to the opening that same night of a new cabaret: the *Cricket*, in the avenue de l'Opéra.

'Sorry,' I said, putting the card back on the table.

'No harm done,' she replied.

I could still smell her perfume as I went down in the lift.

As I stepped out of the lift someone who'd been sitting nearby got up and came over to me. It was Chassard. Definitely difficult to shake off. He looked quite jaunty again.

'No hard feelings,' he said.

'Me neither,' I answered.

'That's OK then.'

'Do you live here?'

'What an idea! I couldn't afford it. I hang out at a little hotel in the rue Saint-Roch.'

'I don't need the details.'

'You're a detective, aren't you? I was waiting to offer you a drink. Are you game?'

'Yes. Have you got some arsenic on you?'

'No, but there's a chemist's shop just round the corner.'

We left practically arm in arm, and went to wet our whistles in a quiet bar in the rue Cambon.

'I suppose you take me for a bit of a cad,' he said.

'Not any more.'

'The thing is – you see what a figure she's got, young Jany? I can't help it, she gets under my skin. I've had my eye on her for a long time, but nothing doing. So when I found out her bloke was a crook . . . '

'How *did* you find out? It wasn't mentioned in the papers.'

'The papers! The news just got around. As I was saying, when I found out her bloke was a crook and had got himself bumped off, I tried my luck.'

'Don't try it any more.'

'All right, all right! But listen . . . I didn't really mean it seriously when I said it, but don't you think it *could* have been her who did him in?'

'The police don't suspect her, according to the papers.'

'The papers! Do *you* believe what they say?'

'No.'

'There you are, then!'

'She's my client.'

'Is or was?'

'Is. You know what that means, don't you? So don't go trying it on with her again.'

'All right – I'll look out for another one a bit like her in the rue Caumartin. Though if I had the money—! Still, I must say . . . I know she's your client, and I wouldn't want to run her down, but I must say this whole business about the picture strikes me as fishy.'

'Did you know Larpent?'

'Only by sight . . . Fancy him pinching something out of a museum! Is there a market for paintings like that?'

'There certainly is.'

'Who buys them?'

'Collectors.'

'How much do they pay?'

'Millions.'

'You seem very well informed.'

'It's all in the papers.'

'The papers!'

He called the barman, ordered more drinks, and swallowed his in one gulp.

'I don't give a damn about the papers,' he muttered. 'But I do give a damn about that tart.'

He gave me a threatening look. He'd taken plenty on board before he came up to see Geneviève Levasseur. Now he was about to keel over.

'You'd do better not to,' I told him. 'Or else change your methods of persuasion.'

His face fell. He looked on the point of tears.

'You'll get to sleep with her,' he said. 'You're older than I am, but you'll get to sleep with her.'

Everybody wanted me to sleep with her, apparently. All right. I'd try. I'm not one to argue.

'I'm younger than you,' he droned on, 'but I seem old, I give off an atmosphere of age, I smell of old hags. You saw through me all right. That's what I live off – old hags. Lousy, rotten, wrinkled old hags that you have to go easy with or else they start falling to pieces. They're only held together with pins and cosmetics. Beauty cream, they call it! I call it ugliness cream. I used to be quite well known round here not long ago. I've had old bats of all descriptions, from ex-pros to duchesses. Old bitches who gave me board and lodging and clothes, but never came across with any money – or none worth speaking of. But I never get to screw with any young ones. They scent me coming a mile off. I smell of old flesh. Perhaps if I had some money . . . But without it . . . I don't know what I wouldn't do to get my hands on some cash.'

I wasn't going to suggest work.

'What about a burglary?'

'I'm too frightened,' he said artlessly. 'It's because I'm always frightened that those horrible old men and women always get the better of me . . . '

'Men?' I queried.

'A slip of the tongue,' he said with a scowl.

'I thought so.'

'Hey, *you* ought to give me a job. I might be a reformed character.'

'But you just admitted you're always afraid!'

'So what? You don't have to be one of the Three Musketeers to trail a bloke or grill a concierge. What *is* a detective's job anyway? Divorces, inquiries, maybe acting as go-between sometimes – but go-between about what? Not anything very dangerous, anyhow. Don't tell me you have to go around with a gun . . . '

'Sometimes.'

'Like Al Capone's bodyguard?'

'Why not?'

'Do you often provide people with bodyguards?'

'Occasionally.'

'You don't think I'd do?'

'I shouldn't think so.'

'Oh well . . . While there's life there's hope. Perhaps, one of these days . . . I'd better go now. I need a whiff of fresh air. No, don't you . . . '

Whether he meant this or not, I made no effort to pay the bill, and he took a few notes out of his wallet. Among the various bits of paper in it I noticed a yellow card – an invitation to the new cabaret.

'Don't go,' I said.

'Don't go where?'

'To that opening. Mlle Levasseur may be there.'

'So what? Am I banned from wherever she chooses to go and waggle her behind?'

'For the time being, yes.'

'What a cheek! . . . Oh well, what the hell! Here, you have the invite – then I shan't be tempted to do what Daddy told me not to.'

I took it, he paid, and when we parted outside the bar I saw him go into another dive. I made tracks to the agency. Hélène was waiting for me.

'At last!' she said. 'Where've you been?'

'With Mlle Geneviève Levasseur.'

'I see! . . . Show!'

'Show what?'

'Your mouth.'

She examined it.

'What, no lipstick?'

'We haven't got to that point yet.'

'But you're on the way?'

'Maybe.'

She pulled a face.

'Oh well, you're of age,' she said. 'Joke over. Now let's be serious. What's all this in the papers? What's been going on here?'

'Is it in the papers?'

'You said it! And the phone hasn't stopped ringing since I got here. Marc Covet's tongue's hanging out.'

'Let it hang. Have you got one of their rags?'

She handed me a copy of the *Crépuscule*. The Birikos affair was all over the front page:

PRIVATE EYE BURGLED
ONE INTRUDER DEAD ON SCENE OF CRIME.

The headlines were huge, but the article was small. I could see why Covet wanted more dope. Hélène too. I was beginning to put her in the picture, if you'll forgive the expression, when Covet called again.

'M. Burma isn't back yet,' Hélène told him, as instructed.

'I'll call back every fifteen minutes then,' he protested. 'I'm bound to get him some time.'

'As you like.'

'You don't know anything yourself?'

'Not a thing.'

That was more or less true, and I set about remedying it.

'All right – joke over,' she said again when I'd finished. A curious funeral oration for the Greek. 'I've come in to give you a report. But I'm wondering whether to chuck up my job with you and get myself taken on in a hotel. It brings in much more money! Young Albert's rolling in it. I trailed him to the races today, and you should have seen what he spent! He must have enough dough to pay all your debts!'

'As much as that? That's very interesting.'

'What's really interesting is the fact that he doesn't seem to have been in easy street for long . . . I don't know why you got me to follow him, but anyhow I noticed that. He betted on practically all the horses, and lost enough shirts to fill the men's department at the Galeries Lafayette. The friends he met at the racecourse couldn't believe their eyes to see him so flush . . . I saw him give money to one or two of them. Money he owed them, presumably.'

'Excellent,' I said. 'I'll look into it. Now I want you to go back to the hotel.'

'For long?'

'I don't think so.'

'Oh, I was forgetting. I put five hundred francs on a horse called Nestor – I couldn't resist. It came in last.'

'That's your business, my sweet. You could easily have followed Albert to the races without betting yourself.'

'Are you serious? It's nothing to do with you?'

'I regard it as a matter of principle.'

'Well, I told you wrong. My horse won.'

'Nestors always win . . . But that puts a different complexion on the matter. Fifty per cent belongs to the agency!'

She thumbed her nose at me and vanished.

I picked up the phone and called Faroux.

'I've got myself into Mlle Levasseur's good graces.'

'Have you indeed! And?'

'It wasn't your spies she was worrying about. It was a kind of gigolo who's had enough of aged flesh and would like a taste of fresh meat. As our young lady didn't find his sex appeal irresistible, he threatened to tell everyone she was the one who murdered Larpent.'

'And then what?'

'And then nothing. I threw the gigolo out, and now I'm on the best of terms with the girl. I'm even quite friendly with the gigolo. He doesn't bear grudges.'

'Maybe we should do something?'

'What?'

'Check her alibis again.'

'If you've got nothing better to do. But if she was guilty she wouldn't have called for help. It would have been easier just to play ball with the gigolo.'

'Women are so complicated . . . '

'Please yourself.'

I rang off, grinning. Silly asses, thinking Geneviève Levasseur had bumped off her lover! Where would they all be without clever little Nestor?

When I got to the hotel in the rue de Valois, Albert was sitting behind the desk studying a racing paper, picking out the wonder nags that were going to run away with his spondulicks. It was a quiet little provincial-type hotel. Not enough comings and goings to disturb the dust on the aspidistra. Albert frowned when he saw me.

'Hallo,' I said.

'Evening, monsieur. Have you . . . have you got any news of M. Lheureux?'

'Yes.'

'Good news?'

'Yes.'

'I'm glad.'

'I'd like to talk to you.'

'Go ahead.'

'Somewhere quiet.'

'Eh?'

'Somewhere where we shan't be disturbed.'

'What's up?'

'Nothing. What makes you think anything's up?'

'I don't know. You look a bit odd.'

'I lost a packet at the races.'

'You're not the only one.'

'Yes, but I can't afford it.'

'Nobody can. And everybody does.'

'That's enough philosophy. Now are we going to that somewhere quiet?'

He stood up, gave me a shifty look, shrugged, and led the way to a little sitting room that had last been aired for the visit of King Alphonse XIII.

'Go on – shoot,' he said. 'I haven't got long.'

'It won't take long. You pinched something from poor old Lheureux, didn't you?'

He made a feeble attempt at protest.

'Now look here—'

'I'm in a hurry . . . '

I grabbed him by the collar and gave him a shake.

'You're coming with me to the cop shop. It's not far. Just round the corner.'

'You wouldn't do that, would you, monsieur?'

'Wouldn't I just!'

'Listen, monsieur . . . Hell! don't shake me about like that – I've just had my dinner.'

I let him go.

'Come on – spit it out.'

He lowered his voice.

'All right – I did take some dough. You'd have done the same if you was me – he was loaded. A hick like him, stingy as the devil with his tips – it didn't seem right he should have all that money. He must be a big shot at home. What does he do? He registers here as a man of independent means.'

'Never mind about what *he* does – just tell me what *you* did. And don't leave anything out!'

'You needn't be so coarse!'

'Never mind about that either! Just spill the beans.'

'Well, when the car sent him flying his case burst open and his wallet was in the middle of it all.'

'Wallet?'

'Yes, wallet. He had too much money to keep it in his pocket. So as well as one wallet in his pocket, he had another one in his case. And when I opened it . . . Oh God! I suppose it couldn't make things any worse if I told you . . . I'd already helped myself from the till here . . . For the horses. So I helped myself from the wallet too. I was quite clever about it, though I say so myself! I did it while I was arranging his shirts and socks and underpants and things!'

'Is that all?'

'Hell! What more do you want? So now go on – call the fuzz!'

'Be quiet!' I said.

I looked deep into his eyes. There was nothing there but funk. Funk because he'd nicked the money from Lheureux and he thought I was going to call the cops.

'You don't look very pleased, after all that,' he said. Then he tried to hide his panic with an attempt at sarcasm. 'I didn't know you were such a stickler for morality! Huh! A private eye who keeps stiffs in his office . . . At least, that's what it says in the papers.'

I went towards the door.

'To hell with the papers, and to hell with morality!' I said.

He stared at me in amazement, then started to giggle nervously. He couldn't get over being let off so lightly.

I went into the café on the corner opposite the Magasins du Louvre, and put in a call to Hélène, disguising my voice.

'Hallo – Ubu speaking!' I said. 'You can quit now.'

'Did you get what you wanted?'

'No. But you can quit just the same. I was on the wrong track. You can go home to bed and come in to the office in the morning.'

'But I've paid for a week in advance. I might as well get my money's worth. It's central here, and I don't have to bother to make my bed.'

'Please yourself.'

When I left the café I bought the latest editions of the papers and went to read them over a meal. I set more store by the papers than I care to admit. I read that a car belonging to Birikos had been found abandoned near Trocadéro. The police hoped to get some fingerprints.

That was all. Fine.

I went back to my own flat to dress up for the opening of the *Cricket*, hoping Larpent's 'widow' wouldn't be deterred from attending by her bereavement.

The phone rang as I was shaving, but I let it ring. It was probably Marc Covet, hungry for a story. But I didn't need him for the moment. And anyway I hadn't got anything to tell him.

Thinking of Louis Lheureux's wallet as I did so, I tidied up my own, as I do about every two years, when the sorting out and whittling down can't be put off any longer. I kept only the absolute minimum – my identity papers and a bit of money. Very slim and elegant. But I knew what I was like: it would soon be bulging again with leaflets, press cuttings, torn-off bits of newspaper with notes written on them, and so on. I got rid of some of the bits and pieces into a drawer: income tax reminders, political pamphlets, receipts from itinerant photographers. There were two photographs: one of me and the other of

Hélène, both masterpieces having been executed during one of our country excursions.

There was also a little transparent sachet that must once have held another photo, but now contained only a few specks of dust. I was just going to throw it away when it occured to me to look for the photograph itself.

Then I noticed the faint traces of the initials 'L.L.' pencilled in one corner of the sachet, and suddenly it all came back to me. The photograph Mme Lheureux had sent to help me identify her husband! What had I done with it? I was sure I hadn't sent it back.

When I'd finished dressing I still had some time to spare, so on the way to the *Cricket* I called in at the agency. There too the phone was ringing, and there too I let it ring. Marc Covet again, no doubt. Finally his persistence must have got on his own nerves and he rang off. Meanwhile I'd consulted the file on Lheureux.

If the photograph I was after ever had been in it, it wasn't in it any more. Was it this that my burglars had fought over so fatally? Very unlikely. As far as I could remember, the file in question had been on a top shelf, where it hadn't been disturbed. But the intruders *might* have got it from my wallet, if it had been there ever since Mme Lheureux's first letter.

'Another mystery, eh?' I said to the telephone, which was now sounding off again.

But it was too late now to solve it, so I put all the stuff away and made tracks, leaving the phone still agonizing.

10 Nice work

The *Cricket* was opening not far from Gilles's cabaret, and for one evening provided it with some stiff competition. Almost all the cars parked along the avenue de l'Opéra and the adjoining streets belonged to the people who'd been invited to the party. I looked like a country bumpkin, going there on foot through the icy drizzle. But then I worked just nearby. Not far from the new place someone was leaning against a wall, sheltering as best he could under a meagre shop awning and gloomily smoking a cigarette. As I approached he gave a short laugh and straightened up.

'Have you changed your mind?'

'What do you mean?'

'Do you wish you hadn't passed on the invitation?'

'I don't give a damn about the invitation. I was just watching the comings and goings. I find it very amusing.'

'Lots of old women among the crowd?'

'Sod you.'

'You'll have to give me some addresses.'

He went pale with anger, but controlled himself with an effort. He shot me a vindictive glance, then shrugged, turned up his coat collar and flung off, attempting to whistle.

I went into the cabaret, left my things in the cloakroom and went downstairs where the floor show was. The atmosphere there was smooth and sumptuous, smelling of expensive perfume, and drink and tobacco to match. With perhaps a whiff of bodies. There was a tiny stage at one end of the room, and the guests were seated round a tiny dance floor. Everything except the glasses they were drinking from was tiny. Just right. I managed to find myself a corner, where I listened to a poor man's Damia singing *Autumn Leaves,* followed by *The Lament of Jack the Ripper* to music by Christiane Verger.

What better way
For a tart to quit the trade
Than when the last client of the night
Stalks through the streets.

Here comes the phantom.
The mist comes down in our hearts.
Here comes the phantom –
The ghost of Jack the Ripper.

The singer made a bow, acknowledging the applause. Her frontage was so ample I was afraid she might not be able to straighten up again. But it was all right. A chap in a dinner jacket took her place and announced that the guests would now be able to dance for a while, thanks to one Pascal Pascal and his orchestra. The band swarmed on to the stage and the hullabaloo began.

Through the changing lights that accompanied the various numbers I scanned the room for Geneviève Levasseur. At last, through a haze of tobacco smoke, I spotted her sitting with friends at a table some distance from mine. But she didn't seem to be enjoying herself very much. It was as if the 'widow' felt obliged to put in an appearance for purely professional reasons. Laugh, Pagliaccio, though your heart is breaking . . . and so on. I made my way over and stopped by her table. She looked up out of her slanting, almost green eyes. They were sparkling, but she gave me a sad little smile.

'Oh! How do you come to be here?'

I returned her smile.

'I'm a Paris celebrity, aren't I?'

'Of course . . . ' she replied. Then she excused herself to her companions and joined me.

'You're a terrible man!' she simpered.

Her evening gown became her like a dream. She was a model, after all. The black sheath dress showed more bare flesh than she'd exhibited a few hours earlier, and she couldn't have been wearing much underneath. But these off-the-shoulder gowns are deceptive. The neck and arms and a considerable amount of back are visible, but the minute whaleboned bodice or whatever you call it – the part that conceals the bosom – that's just a sell. It fits so tight the wearer could turn cartwheels without revealing anything to speak of. A downright fraud, if you ask me.

'Terrible?' I said. 'Why?'

'Never mind. Aren't you going to ask me to dance?'

She put her hand on my arm. Her perfume obliterated all the others.

'Sorry,' I faltered. 'I can't dance.'

'Really?'

'Really.'

'You ought to learn.'

'One of these days. When I have time.'

'Yes . . . '

Her eyes grew misty. She shuddered.

'When your corpses leave you free long enough.'

'Oh! You heard about that? Of course – it was in the papers. Is that why you said I was terrible? It wasn't my fault, you know.'

'Since you can't dance,' she said, changing the subject abruptly, 'you can buy me a glass of champagne at the bar.'

The bar was in a sort of annexe from which you could see the other room, including the stage, through an arch. We went and sat at one end of the counter.

'To think I called you in for some peace and quiet,' she sighed. 'I thought you were a reassuring sort of chap. And then they go and find dead bodies in your office.'

'There's no such thing as peace and quiet,' I said. 'Take your hotel. It's famous and supposed to be respectable, isn't it? Well—'

'I know,' she interrupted. 'And yet Etienne stayed there . . . And . . . and Birikos too . . . '

'The manager must be furious.'

'He doesn't show it, but he must be.'

'Listen, Geneviève – I may call you Geneviève? . . . If not, please don't pay me out by calling me Nestor at the top of your voice! . . . '

With a smile she indicated that I might use her Christian name.

'Well then, Geneviève, you've only got yourself to blame, since you brought the conversation round to him: I want to talk to you about Birikos.'

'Not here, if you don't mind.'

'Just tell me whether you knew him or not.'

At that point a third person intervened and prevented her from answering. An interloper who clapped me on the shoulder and bawled in a voice at least 45 degrees proof:

'Nestor, you old devil!'

I turned to confront the beaming face and watery eyes of Marc Covet, reporter on the *Crépuscule*.

'Lying low then, are we?' he said reproachfully. 'Not answering the phone, always on the move, leaving our friends high and dry?'

'I wouldn't say you were particularly dry.'

'Very witty!'

'Excuse me a moment,' said Geneviève. 'I'll be back.'

'Nice work if you can get it,' said Covet as she went.

'You frightened her away.'

'She said she'd be back. Anyhow . . . I'm very glad to have got hold of you. What's all this Birikos business?'

'Don't you read the papers?'

'I write them, and God only knows it's not always easy. I have a feeling you're not going to tell me anything.'

'Quite right.'

He smiled and frowned at one and the same time.

'All right then. I'll clam up too.'

'Good. You were starting to get on my nerves.'

As I spoke I was scrutinizing the bar, and despite the soft lights and shadows I managed to make out Geneviève at the far end, in conversation with an elderly charmer. They were just separating. Geneviève disappeared in the direction of the washrooms, and I couldn't see the old gent any more.

'I'm off,' said Covet. 'I'll see if I can get a few tips somewhere else.'

Geneviève was making her way back. Covet went up and exchanged a few words with her, then was lost in the crowd.

'I hope I wasn't away too long?' said Geneviève, slipping on to the stool next to mine.

She looked tired and depressed. Was it because she'd talked to Covet? I said something polite about missing her. Then:

'Did he try to get something out of you?'

'Who?'

'That idiotic reporter friend of mine.'

'Maybe . . . But I didn't tell him much.'

She emptied her glass.

'Are you staying on, M. Burma?'

'I don't know.'

'I'm leaving. I can't stand any more of this noise. Will you see me home? You are in a way my body-guard.'

'That reminds me – I saw Chassard lurking about.'

'You see? I need you . . . ' She shrugged. 'Poor old Chassard – he's more to be pitied than anything.'

'You wanted me to pitch him out of the window.'

'Yes. It wasn't a bad idea.'

It was my turn to shrug.

'You go on up,' she said. 'I'll just say goodnight to my friends.'

I paid what I owed and went and collected my outdoor things. She caught me up in the cloakroom, where she collected a fur cape. Her car was parked in the rue des Pyramides, just a short way away. It was a smart little convertible.

'Would you mind driving, M. Burma?'

I got behind the wheel.

'Where to?'

'Where do you think?'

'I don't know.'

'Perhaps to your place, smart guy?'

'No. Too dusty.'

'That's what I thought. So to the Transocean Hotel, please, James. And step on the gas. I'm thirsty.'

'In that case we could stop at a bar, or go back to the *Cricket*.'

'No, I'd rather have a drink at my place.'

'Very good, mademoiselle . . . '

'What do we do with the car?' I asked, when we stopped at the entrance to the hotel.

'The attendants see to that sort of thing,' she said, getting out. 'But perhaps, if you've got a long way to go home . . . ?'

I was still sitting in the car.

'Quite a long way.'

'Would you like to borrow it?'

'Well . . . '

'Is someone waiting up for you?'

'I expect so.'

'You're not sure?'

'Yes. I am sure. Someone *is* waiting.'

'What's her name?'

'Electricity Bill.'

She gave a strained laugh.

'You're priceless!' she said.

'Unfortunately!'

I got out and slammed the door to. It was a very smart little car.

'You shouldn't have made me talk so much. I'm thirsty now too. Can I . . . can I come up for a minute?'

She looked at me without answering, then turned on her heel. I followed in the wake of her perfume. As we passed the desk she asked for refreshments to be brought up to her apartment. Once there she threw her fur cape aside and sank down on her usual wing chair.

'I hope you won't mind my asking you not to stay long, M.Burma,' she said. 'I'm tired out. Take your coat off, though. It's stifling in here.'

I dumped my hat and coat on a chair, on top of her cape.

'Cigarette?'

I took one of the filter tips and lit both hers and mine.

'Did you know Birikos?' I asked.

I was fated to get nowhere with this question. Hardly were the words out of my mouth than there was a knock at the door. It was the tray Mlle Levasseur had ordered, delivered by a sleepy waiter.

'Did you know Birikos?' I asked again, when the flunkey had gone back to bed.

She looked at me over the rim of her glass.

'You really are a detective, aren't you? Questions right away – you don't let the grass grow under your feet. It must be a very fascinating profession – won't you tell me about some of your cases?'

'I don't know. Why should I indulge your morbid curiosity?'

'It's not morbid.'

'Yes, it is. Why do you want to know about other dramas? Isn't the one you're mixed up in enough for you?'

'All right,' she said stiffly. 'I asked for that.'

'Are you offended?'

'No. It's my own fault. I'm very foolish.'

'You're very charming. And I'll tell you plenty of stories about villains – but not now. It would take too long, and there mightn't be time for you to answer my question: did you know Nick Birikos?'

'You are terrible!'

'Frightful.'

'Make fun of me if you like. No, I didn't know him. I know he stayed here, that's all. I must have passed him in the corridor, and he must have bowed to me, like everyone else. Though fewer and fewer people do recognize me now . . . '

She sighed. Then, mockingly:

'Now may *I* ask *you* a question? You asked me if I knew Birikos just because we were both staying in the same hotel. Isn't that rather like asking someone who lives in the rue du Faubourg-Saint-Honoré if he knows the President of France?'

'Is that your question?'

'No. My question is this: did *you* know Birikos, and what was he doing in your office? It wasn't in *my* room that they found his . . . that he died.'

'I didn't know Birikos, and I don't know why he broke into my office. Nor do I know the reason for his death. But I have every reason to believe he knew your lover.'

'I can't be of any use to you there!' she snapped. 'I didn't take any interest in Etienne's . . . business. I don't even know what it was about. The police are the ones who know that.'

'There you go again!' I protested. 'Here we are, enjoying a nice quiet conversation and you have to drag in the police. It's absurd!'

'You're quite right. Let's change the subject.'

I looked at my watch.

'It's getting late,' I said.

'Another half-hour won't make any difference,' she said. 'You can take my car. Drink up!'

I did so, and she refilled my glass.

While she was standing up she put an LP on the turntable. A languorous dance tune, ambiguous as an alibi, started to insinuate its way round the room.

She sat back in her chair, glass in hand, beating time to the music with her foot.

'How is it a man like you doesn't know how to dance?' she said. 'I can't understand it.'

I picked up my glass and emptied it.

'People learn to dance when they're sixteen or seventeen,' I said. 'I had other fish to fry then.'

She slipped off her left shoe and began to stroke first her foot, then her ankle.

'Such as?'

'Perhaps a bit of shop-lifting, to keep body and soul together.'

'What! Nestor Burma, defender of the law, a shoplifter!' She threw back her head and laughed.

'I'm not a defender of the law,' said I. 'Most laws are lousy. I just earn a living, that's all.'

She came over, limping in only one high-heeled shoe.

'Here, have another drink. You're getting bitter – this'll make you more mellow.'

Our fingers touched as I took the glass. The music was still oozing around.

'Such a lovely tune!' she said, putting on her other shoe. 'I'm going to teach you to dance – *now!*'

'You'd better put some boots on, then!' I laughed.

'I'll take the risk.'

She put her arms round me and we executed a few uncertain steps. Not very graceful. Her perfume combined with all I'd been drinking to make my head spin. I could feel her heart beating excitedly against my chest. I brought us to a standstill and clasped her tightly around her bare shoulders.

'M. Burma!' she whispered reproachfully.

'Never mind the "Monsieur"!' I croaked.

'You're hurting me!'

I only held her to me more fiercely, pressing my lips against hers. They smelled of raspberries. She didn't return my kiss. On the contrary, I felt her stiffen as if repelled.

I let go.

'I'm sorry,' I said. 'But it was your fault.'

She tottered over to her chair and collapsed into it, sobbing, her face buried in her arms. I looked at her for a moment in silence, then put on my coat and picked up my hat.

'Goodnight,' I said. 'Goodnight . . . Geneviève.'

She lifted up a face bathed in tears, dabbed at the tip of her nose with a handkerchief she'd fished out from somewhere, and looked at me apprehensively.

She caught me up at the door, and this time it was *she* who imprisoned *me* in her deliciously scented arms. The kiss she gave me now more than made up for the one she'd just refused. The music still swirled sweetly and suggestively around us. I felt as if I was embracing a copy of *Vogue*.

I woke up feeling slightly fragile. I seemed to be lying in a strange bed. I know my own very well: the mattress has lumps in it. This one was as smooth as silk. A streak of pale daylight filtered in between the curtains to show a perfumed bedroom that wasn't mine. I could feel a warm body lying beside me. I turned towards it . . . Geneviève. She stirred, murmured something unintelligible, and went on sleeping.

So that was that! They'd won – Faroux, Chassard and all the prophets! But Faroux had been wrong about one thing. Thirty, he'd said she was. Maybe. But some of those years had counted double. She was still beautiful, but without the help of make-up and lighting her face showed . . . well, it showed her real face. Her bosom too lost much of its pride.

Then I was disgusted with myself. What was I doing, criticizing so cold-bloodedly, and in such circumstances? M. Nestor Burma, detective, was going to turn into an out-and-out swine if he wasn't careful.

I got out of bed, put on my trousers and went into the sitting-room. I switched on the light and saw my reflection in a mirror. M. Nestor Burma, detective. Huh. Noiselessly, methodically, I searched the sitting-room, the bedroom, the bathroom, the wardrobe and the clothes inside it. I looked everywhere. I didn't know what I was looking for, and I didn't find anything, but I pressed on with my lousy job. I wasn't the only one, if that was any consolation. It was plain to an experienced eye that some-one had searched here before, and quite recently. Perhaps the police. Perhaps others.

I was back in the sitting-room when I heard Geneviève calling me. I went into the bedroom.

'Does Mademoiselle wish me to open the curtains so she can contemplate the Tuileries Gardens?' I said.

'Such poetry from a detective!' she cooed. 'No, darling. Please *don't* touch the curtains. I look awful first thing in the morning.'

It didn't sound like affectation. She was really worried about it.

I went back into the sitting-room, drew the curtains, opened the windows and stepped out on to the balcony. The air was icy cold. A yellowish fog hung over Paris. But it would soon be gone. The sun was rising behind the Louvre.

11 The birds

By ten o'clock I was at the office. Hélène was sitting at her typewriter looking through the papers.

She sniffed.

'Where've you been, boss?' she said.

'In bed. Sort of.'

'I thought you must have fallen into a vat of Chanel. You'll need to get that suit disinfected.'

I pointed to the papers.

'Anything new, my love?'

'Pull yourself together. You're in the Fiat Lux Agency, not in your paramour's bed.'

'Anything new anyway?'

'No. Reboul phoned.'

'And?'

'Nothing.'

'What about Zavatter?'

'No news from him.'

'We'll pay him a little visit this afternoon. Just to amuse ourselves.'

'You'd do better to have a rest.'

'What about Covet?'

'Nothing from him. He must have worn the *Crépu*'s phone out yesterday.'

'Faroux?'

'Nothing from him.'

I smoked a pipe, then called the Superintendent.

'Nothing to report,' I told him.

'But you're keeping in contact?'

'You said it!'

'Eh? What?' he gasped. 'No! You don't say! I was only joking.'

'It's no joking matter.'

'True enough! But nothing to tell?'

'Not for the moment. What about you?'

'Our Montparnasse painters have disappeared.'

'What about the Birikos affair?'

'No progress. We still haven't heard from Greece. His car was found abandoned . . . '

'I saw that in the paper.'

'We're examining it for prints and so on. We did come across an address book in his luggage at the hotel, but we haven't found anything significant in it so far. Most of the people have disappeared or died. We've already eliminated some who are still alive, including a shopkeeper on the quai de la Mégisserie. Peltier, his name is. But he's not one of your burglars, and *ipso facto* not Birikos's murderer: he spent the night in question at a birthday party with friends, one of whom is a police inspector. We checked up just the same, because Peltier told us he knew Birikos in the unoccupied zone during the war, and more recently Birikos did him some kind of good turn – to do with money, probably. And we thought: people never forgive a favour . . . '

'And the beneficiary ends up killing the benefactor?'

'Exactly. But we were barking up the wrong tree. Peltier hadn't had anything to do with Birikos for a long time. And he couldn't tell us much about him. As far as he was concerned, Birikos was a rich, eccentric Greek from Athens who occasionally bought a bird with him. But he hadn't bought anything for some while. Anyhow, it wouldn't surprise me if the Athens police told us Birikos was a collector as you suggested. A collector and an eccentric . . . Would it ever occur to you to go buying birds?'

'Well . . . ! Talking of Birikos, Mlle Levasseur didn't know him.'

'And we haven't come across anything to suggest that *he* knew Larpent . . . '

When Faroux rang off, I lit my pipe.

'Peltier,' I murmured. 'Quai de la Mégisserie . . . Hélène,' I said, 'it's nearly midday. It's not very cold. In fact it's quite nice and sunny every now and then. Let's go for a stroll along the quais.'

'Like a couple of lovers.'

'Exactly! I can promise you some fun, anyway.'

The fog was still hanging about. The sun hadn't kept its dawn promise. But every so often it shot out a lazy ray which, pale though it was, brightened everything up. The quais presented their usual spectacle along by the river. Inoffensive citizens rummaging in boxes of books. Sellers of seeds, gardening implements and birds cluttering the pavement with their noisy stalls. I had no difficulty finding Peltier's shop: his name was painted in large green letters over the door. I gave Hélène the bag of sweets we'd bought on the way.

'It's Thursday,' I said.* 'Round up all the kids – boys

* Thursday used to be the school half-holiday in France. It is now Wednesday. (Translator's note.)

and girls – that you can find in the neighbourhood. Rich, poor, well dressed or in rags – it doesn't matter. Gather them all together opposite our man's shop.'

'What are you going to do, boss?'

'You told me to rest, didn't you? Well, I *am* going to relax. A private eye can't spend all his time juggling dead bodies. Sometimes he needs a bit of poetical recreation.'

Hélène went off in search of the urchins, and I walked towards the shop. I could see a chap in a once-white overall making up to a customer inside. After a while a noise on the opposite pavement alerted me to the fact that Hélène had managed to collect a crowd of young spectators. A couple of dozen of them were jabbering to one another, their cheeks bulging with sweets. I signed to Hélène and went into the shop, where the bird-seller was showing his customer out. He glanced curiously at the bunch of kids across the road, then came over to me.

'Can I help you, monsieur?'

'Is your name Peltier?' I asked.

'Yes.'

'Mine's Burma. Nestor Burma. It was at my place that Birikos was killed. You knew him, didn't you?'

'Yes, monsieur, but—'

'He did you a good turn, didn't he?'

'I don't see—'

'And you returned the favour?'

'Listen, monsieur—'

'No, you listen to me, Peltier. Birikos needed to search my place when I wasn't there, and as he could neither kill me, nor imprison me in his hotel, he thought your place would be a good solution. I don't suppose he told you his reasons, but that's neither here nor there. He asked you to lend him your premises to stow me away. And let me tell you I don't like that at all.'

His face went the same colour as his overalls. Dirty white.

'Listen,' he whined. 'Yes, he did want to use the room at the back of the shop. I couldn't refuse. I didn't know – I didn't *ask* him what for. I just gave him the keys. And afterwards I found them left in the door – just think, I might have been burgled! But I hadn't any idea what it was all about, M. Burma. I hadn't, I swear!'

'I still don't like it. Birikos was a wrong 'un. At least, that's the conclusion I came to from his behaviour to me. And for all I know you may be a wrong 'un, too. And the police may be interested to hear that you lent Birikos your place to imprison, bind and gag a private detective. What do you think, bird man? You look like a dying duck.'

'Are you . . . are you going to call the police?'

'You don't like the idea of being shut up in a cage, eh? Did you ask your birds if *they* were keen on it? . . . Don't worry, I'm *not* going to call the cops. That's not my style. You weren't with Birikos when he searched my office, and you didn't kill him. You were just the left luggage office. That doesn't concern the police – it's just between you and me. If the police do come it'll be because *you*'ve called them. And if you do call them, I'll tell all.'

I pointed to a large aviary full of little birds.

'What are they?'

'Goldfinches.'

Suddenly he understood, and tried to jump me. I brushed him aside.

'Go on, Peltier – call the cops. If you've got the cheek!'

I opened all the cages one after the other. The whole shop filled with the rush of wings. Birds of all shapes and sizes fluttered to and fro, crashing into one another, squawking and screeching at the tops of their voices, no doubt more frightened than delighted by their sudden freedom. Never mind, they'd learn. Come on, pals! No more bars, no more skimpy perches, no more idiots whistling and poking dirty fingers at you! I flung the shop door open wide and waved my arms encouragingly. This way! Come on! The birds streamed out like a long multicoloured scarf, and the kids gathered round Hélène on the other side of the street jumped up and down for joy by the river. Their cheers rose up among the trills with which the birds rediscovered the brisk, reviving, inexhaustible air.

Peltier moaned and tore his hair, but it didn't occur to him for a moment to call the cops. The birds scattered over the Paris sky as it was briefly lit up by a burst of sun. Peltier groaned. The swings still rocked gently to and fro inside the empty cages.

I went over to Hélène. Her lovely grey eyes brimmed with tears of delight.

But there was no point in deluding ourselves. It had been a nice little interlude, but I had a strong feeling the nastiness was about to start up again.

12 Indiscretions

We had lunch nearby and then walked along by the river. I had a vague intention of taking Hélène to see Corbigny's yacht, but it didn't work out that way. The sight of some *clochards* making themselves a kind of shelter out of packing cases under the Pont-Neuf reminded me of those who'd taken charge of me that night after my involuntary stay among the birds.

Scraps of what the woman tramp had said now came back to me. 'I know that man,' she'd told Bébert, and she didn't mean me. She must have meant the man in the photograph they'd found in my wallet – the photograph of Louis Lheureux! So it hadn't been filched by Birikos and Co. – the woman tramp had kept it herself, for sentimental reasons. And now it struck me that she must have been the woman Lheureux rebuffed one night the previous year, when we were gallivanting about together in Les Halles.

Aurélienne d'Arnétal, she said she'd been called in the days of her glory.

'Does the name Aurélienne d'Arnétal mean anything to you?' I asked Hélène, as we leaned over the parapet of the Pont-Neuf. (I must have caught the habit from Florimond Faroux.)

'*Who?*'

'She's a tramp now. But in the second Belle Epoque, in the 1920s, she was one of the modern equivalents of great courtesans like Liane de Pougy and Emilienne d'Alençon—'

'You're very well up on these ladies.'

'Aurélienne, in her cups, gave me a hint that I was trying to follow up yesterday in the library. I didn't find what I was looking for, though; I couldn't remember all she said – I wasn't at my brightest when I heard it.'

'Is it important?'

'It just confirms something I'd been wondering about. More important, I understand now why Birikos and Co. thought I was mixed up in the Raphael theft. Come along – I'll see if I can introduce you to Aurélienne d'Arnétal.'

We went down on to the bank of the river, but I couldn't find the deposed queen of Paris anywhere.

Back on street level again I bought a copy of the first edition (masquerading as the sixth or seventh) of the *Crépu*. When I glanced at page one I nearly jumped out of my skin.

There, completely eclipsing politics both foreign and domestic, was a large portrait of Geneviève, exuding sex-appeal from every pore. And there were plenty of them on show.

Marc Covet had me shown into his office straight away. He was smiling sardonically.

'And what's this, may I ask?' said I, brandishing the paper.

As soon as I'd seen it I'd abandoned Hélène, hailed a taxi and had the driver take me straight to the *Crépu* office:

I proposed to give my young friend a piece of my mind.

The headline ran:

THE ADVENTURES OF JANY, PARIS MODEL
LOVELIER THAN THE PAINTINGS IN THE LOUVRE.

The article, credited to Marc Covet, took up half of page two, and rambled on about Geneviève's beginnings, her stint in films, her lovers named and unnamed. There were plenty of anecdotes – some true, some false, all juicy. Etienne Larpent was the lover given the most prominence. Covet kept on bracketing him with Arsène Lupin, the gentleman crook created by Maurice Leblanc. He also referred to Larpent's tragic death and his probable involvement in the theft of the Raphael from the Louvre. From there he went on to talk about Virgins, true and false, wise and foolish. Then from them back to Geneviève, as if there were any connection. Gutter press journalism of the transatlantic variety. Garnished with plenty of sauce and peppered with howlers.

'What's this?' I said.

'Rather good, eh? I'm quite pleased with it.'

'Well, I'm not!'

'Why not? . . . Oh, I see!'

He laughed.

'You were like all the rest of them – you didn't know the gorgeous Geneviève used to be the girlfriend of Larpent, the pilferer of paintings. And while that interesting detail doesn't matter much to anyone else, it's different for you because you *know* the lady. If you'd been nicer to me last night when I asked you about Birikos, I might have told you then.'

'Never mind about that. You may be in for trouble with all this tripe.'

'Oh no. Apart from a few anecdotes about Larpent that I lifted from Leblanc, it's all true . . . '

He paused, and went pale.

'But of course . . . Hell, Burma – you know her better than I do. Is she one of those unscrupulous bitches who'll stop at nothing?'

'No.'

'Phew, thank goodness! Because some of them will tell you a whole rigmarole, beg you to print it, and then turn round and sue!'

'You mean to say—'

'She gave me an interview. The article has her backing.'

'Did she actually suggest it to you?'

'I did see her. But the deal itself was made through a third party – a chap who seemed to me to be making a bit of cash out of it on the sly. Nothing unusual about that, though.'

'This chap you mention . . . '

I described Maurice Chassard.

'That's him,' said Covet.

I told him his name.

'You seem to know all the family,' he grinned.

'He makes no attempt at concealment.'

'Why should he?'

'Why indeed? . . . Well, I suppose it's no use asking you for any more information?'

'Absolutely not,' he smiled. 'For once the boot's on the other foot.'

'See if I care.'

'Good. So we're all happy.'

'Can I use the phone? Then I shan't have wasted my time entirely.'

'Help yourself. It's on the firm.'

I called the Transocean. Geneviève wasn't there. I

looked up Roldy's in the phone book. Roldy, Haute Couture, Place Vendôme. I asked to speak to Geneviève.

'Nestor Burma here.'

'Hallo, darling.'

'I'd like to see you.'

'But of course, my darling,' she cooed. 'I was just about to go home. I'm so tired.' She yawned languorously. 'So tired . . . '

'I'm tired too. I'll be with you right away.'

'See you soon then, darling. Kiss kiss.'

'Kiss kiss, my pet.'

I hung up.

Covet goggled.

'Eh?' he gasped.

'That's right,' I said.

His watery eyes nearly popped out of their sockets.

'Well, I'm damned!' he said.

'That's right,' said I.

She was wearing a diaphanous négligée which put me off my stroke at first. She threw her scented arms around me and held out her ruby lips.

'Darling,' she whispered. 'Are you so eager to see me again?'

'Very eager,' I said, disengaging myself. '*Crépu*! Latest edition! Read all about it!'

I threw the paper at her.

'What's all this?'

'You ought to get married,' she said. 'You behave just like a husband.'

'What *is* it?'

'Publicity,' she said, suddenly serious.

'Crap, more like,' I answered.

'Don't be vulgar.'

'What are all these revelations in aid of? I know you authorized them. None of the papers have mentioned you in connection with this scandal. Even the police seemed to be leaving you out of it—'

'Of course they're leaving me out of it. I should hope so! It's nothing to do with me. Etienne is the guilty party. But guilty of what? We don't even know! But he *was* found dead, and I *was* his girlfriend. And so . . .'

'And so what?'

'A bit of scandal makes a person seem younger.'

'What!'

'Don't you see?'

Her face went limp under the careful make-up.

'I feel as if I were getting old. Rejected. Forgotten. I don't make as many conquests as I did in the past. The quite recent past. And so . . . And so I thought I might turn the fuss about Etienne to my own advantage. At first I intended to keep out of it. Then I started to think . . . It had been a long time, too long, since there'd been anything about me in the papers. The opportunity was too good to miss.'

'Some people pay *not* to get into the papers.'

'But I have nothing to lose. I'm innocent. It isn't even a real scandal. It's rather romantic, really. It can't do me anything but good.'

I shrugged.

'Well, it's all one to me. It can't make any difference . . .'

'What do you mean, darling?'

'Nothing.'

She gazed at me humbly.

'Perhaps I shouldn't have done it . . . But still, what's done is done, isn't it?'

'Was it your idea or Chassard's? Don't pretend to be surprised – I know Chassard contacted the reporter responsible for this masterpiece.'

'I wasn't pretending to be surprised. It was my idea, but Chassard made the arrangements.'

'So it was a good thing I didn't take you at your word and heave him out of the window.'

'Now now, my love. Maurice hasn't got any harm in him. I was scared at first when he tried to blackmail me, but you know what I said yesterday – when you came I wasn't frightened any more.'

'You don't know *what* you want, eh? A real little bird-brain. Do you at least know you slept with me last night?'

She flinched, and gave me a look that was both angry and hurt.

'Are you reproaching me?'

'I thought you might have forgotten. There's no mention of it in the article.'

'That was written before . . . I—'

She was interrupted by the telephone.

'It's for you.' She held it out. 'A woman.'

'Hallo,' I said.

'Hallo, boss,' said Hélène's voice.

'A real little detective,' I snarled.

'One does one's best. I rang Marc Covet, and he told me Mlle Levasseur was at the Transocean. Did I get you out of bed?'

'I'm not in the mood for joking.'

'Neither is Faroux. He wants you to go to see him or ring him up straight away. He sounds fit to be tied.'

'Right. I'll phone him from the office. I'll be there in a few minutes.'

'Take enough time to put your clothes on properly.'

I hung up.

'Mustn't let domestic scenes make me neglect my work,' I said to Geneviève. 'I'm needed at the office.'

She kissed me.

'Goodbye, darling. You're not cross, are you?'

'No.'

'Until this evening . . . perhaps?'

'Until this evening.'

We arranged the time and place, and I left her.

I spotted Chassard in the Place Vendôme. He was crossing over, threading his way through the parked cars, and I was on the pavement. I was about to call out to him, but decided against and followed him instead. He walked in the direction of the Transocean, but stopped under the arcades and hung about by the hotel entrance. I laughed to myself. Perhaps he'd arrived too early. I turned back towards the agency, a nasty taste in my mouth. Poor old Nestor! No use asking the impossible. An expensive négligée like that had to be put to some useful purpose!

Hélène was on the telephone when I arrived.

'Ah, here he is!' she said into the phone. Then, handing it to me: 'Faroux.'

'Hallo,' I began.

'Wipe the lipstick off your face first,' said Hélène.

'I haven't got any lipstick on my face!' I replied.

'I don't give a curse whether you've got any lipstick on your face or not!' yelled Faroux.

'Sorry, Florimond. I wasn't talking to you.'

'Right. Have you seen the *Crépu*?'

'Yes.'

'What does it mean?'

'It means Geneviève Levasseur is crazy . . . '

And I explained why she'd authorized the article.

'Hmm,' said Faroux, 'I was beginning to wonder . . . I must say, though – we do our best to let her off lightly, and all of a sudden she herself goes and . . . People are going to ask why we've never mentioned her before.'

'People don't believe a word of what they read in the papers.'

'Maybe . . . As the piece was by Covet I thought you might have decided to take a hand yourself.'

'You know that's not my style.'

'That's why I was worried,' he said with heavy irony. 'I said to myself: it's not like Nestor to interfere. Nestor would never do a thing like that. But no harm in reminding him of the fact. Get me?'

'I can't help it if she's crazy.'

'You certainly can't cure her. You must make a good couple if she's as loony as that. For God's sake don't have any children! . . . Well, that's all for now. Just one piece of advice: no nonsense, please. No crap.'

'That word keeps cropping up today.'

'There's a lot of it about.'

He rang off, and I called Covet at the *Crépu*.

'Me again,' I said.

'About the Birikos affair?' he said cheekily.

'No, the Geneviève Levasseur affair.'

'Please refer to our extra-special edition!'

'That'll do. How long had you had the piece? Several days?'

'Maybe.'

'And did you talk to her about it yesterday evening at the *Cricket*?'

'We-e-ll . . . ' He obviously wasn't going to tell me anything.

'Go jump in the lake!' I snarled.

I slammed the phone down.

'You're very irritable,' said Hélène. 'Trouble with your love life?'

'Everyone's gone crazy,' I said.

'That reminds me – there's a letter from Zavatter.'

It was on the same luxurious paper as before, with the *Red Flower of Tahiti* letterhead. It ran:

'Report number . . . Gosh boss, I've forgotten. Anyway, whatever number it is, the report's the same as ever. Nothing to tell. All quiet on the western front. Still no enemies in sight. The client's as barmy as ever, but though he was on edge when we got to Paris he seems a bit more serean now. (That doesn't look right.) Anyhow, he's better. Maybe it's because of the medal or charm or whatever it was he bought this afternoon. I don't know exactly – I only waited for him outside the shop. This is what happened. Just after midday he said "Come with me" very mysteriously – you'd have thought he was taking me off to kill someone. We went to the Palais-Royal, and he dived into one of those shops where they sell medals and decorations. "Wait outside," he says, "and keep an eye out for me through the window." The usual daft caper – of course I didn't have to kill anyone and no one killed me. Nobody killed anybody. The client came out again pleased as Punch . . .

Right. I've nearly filled both sides of the page. That's quite enough for a report with nothing in it.

Best wishes.
Roger'

'More crap,' I said. 'Hélène, put this away in the Corbigny file, please.'

'OK, boss. All these letters and reports are quite point-less, but I like things to be neat and tidy. Have you got the other one?'

'The other what?'

'The other letter from Zavatter. The one that came a few days ago.'

'I put it in that drawer.'

'It's not there now,' said Hélène.

'It must be. Have a good look. It's not the crown jewels – no one would want to steal it . . . Oh my God!'

I started to rummage through the drawer – one of the drawers that had been left open the other night, when I found Nick Birikos's body. Zavatter's letter wasn't there. Hélène and I looked everywhere. It was nowhere to be found.

'Vanished,' said Hélène.

'Vanished,' said I, 'because one of the burglars must have taken it. It was that scrap of paper that they quarrelled over, and it was because of that pointless letter that Birikos died. But it wasn't pointless at all – it was the beginnings of a clue. How's this for a theory, Hélène? . . . Birikos and X think I'm involved in the business about the picture. They come here to find a clue. X finds the letter, which puts him on what he thinks is the right track, and decides to keep it to himself. Birikos sees him slipping something into his pocket. He pulls his gun and tells X to hand over. They fight, and Birikos bites the dust.'

'But it doesn't make sense.'

'Nor does a rich guy who pretends to be interested in poetry and philosophy.'

I grabbed my hat and got a taxi to drive me hell for leather to where the *Sunflower* bobbed up and down at its moorings.

The same freshwater tar with his jersey, cap and short clay pipe stood on deck looking vaguely in the direction of the Leeward Islands. I climbed aboard, pushed past the phoney sailor and opened the cabin door. Inside was old man Corbigny, looking rather euphoric, and Zavatter, who jumped up with his hand to his holster, no doubt taking me for the enemies he'd been employed to repel. On the table were some newspapers, together with a bottle and glasses.

'M. Burma!' exclaimed Corbigny. 'This *is* a pleasant surprise! What fair wind blows you here?'

'I wanted to show you how clever I am. If ever you have a problem, you can always apply to me.'

'Good, good . . . M. Zavatter, would you mind pouring us a drink?'

'How's this?' I said. 'You're a rich man, and an expert on art history. You own two boats, one called the *Red Flower of Tahiti* and the other the *Sunflower*.'

Corbigny nodded.

'The name of the first is a tribute to Gaugin – a reference to motifs in his work. The name of the second is a similar tribute to Van Gogh.

'Now although you have refined tastes, you're cynical. And a collector. One of those collectors whose passion for art has stifled his scruples. You left your châteaux in Normandy to come and take delivery of something in Paris. Something very expensive that you couldn't pay for by cheque. And the people you had to pay were not only unscrupulous, like you, but also dangerous. So you needed a bodyguard to protect the cash you were carrying around. And also to protect *you* when you handed it over in exchange for the Raphael stolen from the Louvre. Am I right?'

13 The charms of the Palais-Royal

Roger Zavatter let out a long and heart-felt oath, but M. Pierre Corbigny remained unmoved. He took a sip of his drink.

'Fantastic!' he said. 'How did you find out?'

'By mistake. Somebody else's mistake. Made by a man called Birikos and another man whose name I don't know. They seem to have been accomplices of friend Larpent. *His* death must have upset you, M. Corbigny.'

'Yes,' he admitted. 'I didn't know the gentleman, but I realized his death would complicate things.'

'Birikos, because of my profession and its doubtful reputation, took me to be an intermediary between the thief and the buyer. He tried to pump me, but naturally didn't get any result. So then he and his pal came and searched my office at night, and the pal found one of M. Zavatter's reports, written on paper with a letterhead depicting a boat. This man didn't know anything about the person who was going to buy the picture, except that he owned some boats and didn't live in Paris. The report was obviously written by a bodyguard. So our unknown puts two and two together. Here's a rich man arriving in Paris just when the purchaser is due; he arrives by boat;

and employs a bodyguard, probably to protect a large sum of money.'

Corbigny helped himself to a cigar.

'How come this unknown hasn't been to see me yet?'

'Because you're on the *Sunflower*, and the letterhead on the report depicted the *Red Flower of Tahiti*, which you didn't use because it broke down. And our unknown is just a crook – he doesn't know enough about art to work out the connection.'

'He could have gone round all the boats asking for me.'

'No, because the report refers to you only as "the client" – it doesn't mention your name. That's a precaution we always take. Roger shouldn't really have used your writing paper . . . '

Zavatter scratched his chin.

'But in the circumstances I'll overlook it.'

'I won't!' cried Corbigny. 'He ought to have given my name in full! My name, age, waist measurement, and the hours when I'm at home to visitors. Then the man you're talking about would have been here already!'

'Better not,' I said.

'Look here, Burma,' said he sharply. 'If I want to buy that picture, *you*'re not going to stop me. You're not a real cop. If this man's got the painting—'

'But he hasn't. I know. Larpent made use of accomplices, but he kept control of things in his own hands. The others didn't know who either the buyer or the go-between was. The surviving accomplice hasn't got the picture. But you, M. Corbigny, you've got some millions of francs in cash somewhere handy, and he's going to want to get hold of it. One more corpse won't bother him. He'll kill you as soon as look at you.'

Corbigny looked worried.

'Fortunately I've got M. Zavatter.'

'M. Zavatter doesn't *have* to go on protecting you. Come now, M. Corbigny, forget about the picture. Your life's in danger. This chap's looking for you, and in the end he'll find you.'

This wasn't absolutely certain, now that Corbigny had been warned, but it was just as well he should think so.

'If Zavatter's not here you've had it. For my part, I mean to try to find the painting. Perhaps the go-between can put me on the right track . . . '

'He's as much in the dark as I am,' said Corbigny. 'Or rather he was.'

'You mean you've seen him?'

'Yes.'

'When?'

'Yesterday.'

'In the Palais-Royal, eh?'

He didn't answer.

'What's his name?'

'It's none of your business.'

'All right. Zavatter knows the shop. He can show me where it is. Because I'm taking him away with me. Come on, Roger, we're off.'

'Hey, wait!' cried Corbigny. 'Don't go like that! Supposing this chap . . . '

'I thought you *wanted* him to come?'

He glared.

'I've changed my mind. But I don't want to unleash you on my go-between, because there's a ray of hope for me now in that direction.'

'Since yesterday?'

'Yes.'

'What sort of hope?'

'I'll have to wait, apparently, but it'll all come right in the end. The go-between has been given assurances. Larpent's death is a nuisance, but apparently it isn't an insuperable problem.'

'I'm not surprised.'

'I wonder what *would* surprise you,' he sighed.

'It would surprise me if you refused to tell me the name of your go-between.'

He shrugged and gave in.

'Miret,' he said. 'Octave Miret. He's an antique dealer, and sells medals and decorations. In the arcades of the Palais-Royal, as you know. A little way along the Galerie Montpensier . . . '

And he gave me the number without more ado. I left Zavatter to look out for squalls on the yacht, and went off myself to confront the double dealer.

The Palais-Royal was its usual self. Like a chilly provincial graveyard. The garden was closed, and it was growing dark under the arcades. My footsteps echoed hollowly on the paving-stones. The big wrought-iron lamps shed a meagre yellow light. Only a few of the shops were still open. An icy wind blew in from the narrow exits. I wonder what makes anyone find this place attractive. When I think that Colette and Cocteau, and a lot of other writers, artists and people supposed to be educated and intelligent, congratulate themselves on living there. Oh well, every man to his taste. Personally, I know I'd end up committing suicide if I lived there. It's so depressing. Even the memories it evokes are far from cheerful. Partly because they *are* memories, and partly because they're dreary anyway. Gamblers. Prostitutes. Pierre-François Lacenaire coming out of a gambling joint where Benjamin Constant's nephew had convicted him of cheating, and clutching in his pocket the crucifix with a blade attached with which he later killed his accuser. Not to mention the file with which he avenged himself on other miscreants.

On second thoughts I take back what I said just now. The best thing about the Palais-Royal is its sordid, voluptuous and bloody memories.

Right. With all that, I still hadn't located M. Octave Miret's boutique. I found it at last – I hadn't noticed it before because it hadn't got any lights on. The window was filled with serried ranks of medals, decorations and other gewgaws. Enough to decorate all our generals, even if we lost the next war. But was the owner in, or would I have to come back? The handle was still in the door, and when I turned it and entered I set off a little chime of bells. The light suddenly came on, dazzling me, and a man emerged from behind a suit of armour that guarded the entrance to an inner room. He was quite tall, with heavy features, white hair and the general appearance of an ageing beau. Most of the characters in this case were pretty ancient, not to mention the Raphael itself.

'Monsieur Miret?' I said.

'Yes.'

'I'm Nestor Burma.'

'Glad to meet you.'

'That's as may be. Are you alone?'

'Yes.'

'Not expecting any customers?'

'Why all these questions?'

'I want to speak to you in private. Five minutes, that's all.'

I went to the door, detached the handle and let down the blind. No one could see in from the outside now.

No one could see us having a nice quiet conversation at gunpoint.

'You're done for, monsieur,' I told him. 'You'll have to flog all your gongs and get out. Unless you're prepared to be reasonable. By the way, does this medal business bring in very much?'

'What business is it of yours?'

'Peanuts – that's what it brings in. Your main source of income is dealing in stolen property – paintings and other such baubles.'

'I think I'd better call the police,' he said icily.

'That's a good idea. I wonder I didn't think of it myself. Yes, call the police, and I'll tell them how Larpent – I don't know if the name reminds you of anything – how Larpent got you to . . . But no, perhaps that's not the right way to begin.'

'Are you making this up as you go along?' he sneered.

'Of course. But aren't you going to call the police? Go ahead. By the time they get here I'll have thought of some better ways of putting it. For example: one day a wealthy and fanatical collector called Pierre Corbigny, at present aboard his yacht, the *Sunflower*, moored in the Port du Louvre, says to Miret, who must already have sold him stolen art treasures in the past, "There's a certain Raphael I'd like to add to my collection." Miret goes along with that. The business will be worth several hundred million, and some of that's bound to stick to the go-between. For Miret *is* only the go-between. He passes on the orders and delivers the goods. It's Larpent who actually organizes the theft. And I don't think Larpent pinched the picture himself – he must have used an expert. But that's only a detail.'

'You seem to know a good deal!' said Miret.

'Not really,' I answered modestly. 'Not really.'

'What else would you like to know, then?'

'I'd like to know where the painting is.'

'Don't you know that?'

'Not yet. I'll have found out in a couple of days. But I'm impatient. I could find out straight away by telling the police something I've been keeping from them. But I don't like the idea – and I might find myself cut out if I did that. I'd rather find the picture myself and hand it to the cops on a plate. Because of the reward. I suppose you knew there was one? For me it's a matter not only of vanity but also of realism. So I thought to myself that perhaps you might help me.'

'My dear fellow,' he said. 'We're both wasting our time. I won't quibble – I admit all you've said about me is true. But as for the picture itself – believe me I'm as sorry as you are when I tell you I don't know where the damn thing is.'

'Really? I—'

I broke off and jumped. I'd heard a suspicious noise from the inner room. I shoved the medieval jouster out of the way – he bit the dust in true chivalric style – drew aside the curtain over the doorway, and burst into a veritable shambles filled with Miret's stock-in-trade. There was no light except what came in from the shop itself, but by that I could see a man starting to escape down some stairs. I had no difficulty collaring him – it was so easy it felt as if he must be either a cripple or a coward – but then he broke free, flailing away with his hands and his feet. I staggered back on to an antique chair, but it turned out to be too fragile for a citizen of the twentieth century. I thought the other chap would take advantage of my fall to get away properly this time. But no. He just stood by the stairs and looked at me.

'Gentlemen, gentlemen,' pleaded Miret. 'Not here, please! We can talk it over, we can come to some arrangement . . . '

He switched the light on. The other chap was levelling a large gun at me.

'Hands up!' he said.

'Good God!' I exclaimed. 'If it isn't our little old poofter-cum-gigolo, Chassard!'

'Shut your jaw and put your hands up!' he growled.

I obeyed, shedding the débris of the period chair.

'That'll do, my pretty,' I said. 'The sooner you drop that gun the better. You handle it as if it was dynamite. I shouldn't be surprised if you did *yourself* an injury.'

'Belt up!'

'Gentlemen, gentlemen!' Miret implored.

His smooth pink face was almost grey by now.

'You belt up too!' Chassard told him.

'Make up your mind, chum,' I said. 'Are you going to kill me or aren't you?'

I'd been stealthily manoeuvring myself along by the wall to where I might pick up some piece of bric-a-brac and throw it in his kisser. The silly chump didn't even notice. What he was most afraid of was the gun in his hand.

'Why shouldn't I kill you?' he hissed. 'You wouldn't be the first!'

'Baloney. Tell me exactly where their gravestones are in the cemetery. Otherwise I won't believe you.'

I'd moved a few inches nearer. I froze.

'The one I killed hasn't been buried yet. It's that lousy son-of-a-bitch, Birikos . . . '

'Oh, hell!' I said.

'No, no!' howled Miret.

No? Why not? On the contrary, yes!

There's someone behind me, isn't there? Someone whose presence I'm aware of only too late. But you mustn't get excited and shout like that, M. Miret – you'll give Chassard a heart attack.

What you have to understand once and for all is that when someone comes up behind Burma there's a neat little thump in the offing from a truncheon or an axe-handle or a frying-pan, or some other blunt instrument. Any reader of detective stories will tell you that. So don't try to interfere. I'm used to it. This time there's a bonus. I'm being chloroformed as well. Goodnight, Chassard. Goodnight, Miret. Goodnight, everybody, goodnight . . .

14 A toast to an old master

Darkness, darkness. The red light had gone on too late, and all was pitch black. Waves of pain shot from my neck down my spine as if they were sliding down the banisters, and then branched out into my legs. Hell, it was dark! Open your eyes, I told myself. That was an idea. A good idea. A Nestor Burma idea, the sort that doesn't come to just anyone. I did open my eyes. With difficulty. Only more darkness. But it wasn't all dark – there was a glow-worm in it. I was cold. My head was boiling, but not my feet. I tried to catch the glow-worm. I was covered with a lot of small objects that tinkled to the floor when I moved. All of a sudden the glow-worm was right under my nose. It was my watch. Seven o'clock. Morning or evening? Evening, probably. I struggled to my knees, scattering more tin cans, if that was what they were, in the process. I managed to get to my feet. Darkness still. Dizziness. A little light on the subject, please. Fiat Lux, as you might say. I groped for the light switch, and found it after stumbling over more ironmongery. Dazzled, I retrieved my hat from nearby and pulled it over my eyes. Then I looked down at my feet. They were in good shape. They might be able to get me out of this spot. The floor was covered with medals, decorations and suchlike – crosses of the Legion of Honour, crosses of this, that and the other. I could have found a use for a couple of little wooden ones. I stepped over first Miret and then Chassard, and went to see if there was a kitchen or somewhere else with a tap on the premises. I didn't find a kitchen, but I did come across a bottle of brandy. I had a swig of that and felt better. I had another swig and felt almost all right. I went back and took a look in the shop and in the room at the back of the shop. Octave Miret wouldn't be handling stolen goods any more. Maurice Chassard wouldn't need to flatter any more old ladies now, or fall in with the whims of dubious Levantines. A couple of bullets each, and a lot of problems were solved. There was a letter sticking out of Miret's pocket. Ordinary envelope. Ordinary paper. Ordinary letter:

'*Dear Sir*

We regret that owing to circumstances beyond our control we cannot deliver the goods at the time arranged, but would like to assure you we shall fulfil your esteemed order in due course.

Yours etc.'

The signature was illegible.

The form may have been ordinary enough, but the content was not. The letter was probably intended to string Miret along and then, through him, Corbigny. It was typed, but very badly. I put it in my pocket and contemplated the two bodies. You see, my late fine feathered friends? The bad guys are always punished. It's only the goodies that escape. Like Nestor Burma, for example . . . But suddenly I went cold. Why was I here?

If the killer had spared me it couldn't have been for the good of my health. He might have called the police. The characters involved in this business were fond of doing that. Get going, Nestor! And fast! I looked at myself in the glass and didn't much care for what I saw. There was blood on my collar, my coat and my face. I must have touched them all unconsciously while I was sorting myself out. But this wasn't the moment for a wash and brush-up. I found a large duffel-coat in a wardrobe and put it on over my own things, pulling the hood down as far as it would go. Then switched out all the lights and left the shop via the Galerie Montpensier. The Palais-Royal was still painfully peaceful.

I didn't go far. My strength failed me in the Place du Théâtre-Français. I leaned against a pillar under the medallion of Mounet-Sully. Heavy traffic rushed past just a few yards away. The car horns felt to me like so many blows. The footsteps of passers-by thumped on the inside of my skull as if it was the skin of a drum. I was engulfed by all the racket, now near, now far; it was like being on some horrible swing. My ears buzzed. There were spots before my eyes. I was in a bad way – as bad as Alfred de Musset at the other end of the colonnade, only he's made of stone and enjoys the assistance of his Muse, hovering over him like the nurse in the aspirin advertisement. His Muse . . . aspirin . . . Hélène . . . No! I mustn't pass out. Not now. Not here.

I didn't want to go to the agency – Faroux might be there for all I knew. I didn't want to take a taxi. I didn't want to . . . God, all these people! Some Good Samaritan was bound to notice how groggy I looked and call the cops. I steeled myself. Only a hundred yards, Nestor. Not exactly the Marathon. Come on, make yourself walk another hundred yards. I set off to cover them, in slow motion.

Rue de Valois. Albert's hotel. Lheureux's hotel. It took me two attempts to find the door, and I knocked against the wall as I negotiated it. I clutched at the reception desk. Albert stood behind it and gaped. A red mist floated before my eyes.

'Hélène Chatelain,' I croaked.

'What, you here again?'

His voice reached me faintly, through ten miles of cottonwool.

'Shut up! Hélène Chatelain!'

'What on earth's the matter?'

'Hélène Chatelain, for God's sake! Hélène Chatelain's room!'

A sarcastic laugh started a long way away, then came and exploded in my ears.

'Gave you a good working over, did they? – you can't expect everyone to be a little whippersnapper like me! Can't always have it your own way! Where was it you copped it, tough guy?'

I mustered all my strength and swung at him. He wasn't expecting it and I caught him right on the nose. It started to bleed.

He swore.

'Put a sock in it, you stupid sod!' I groaned.

Not very elegant, but brief and to the point.

'Call the cops or Hélène Chatelain.'

'She's not in.'

'Her key, then.'

He held it out, but not to me. To someone who'd just come in. Someone into whose arms I gently collapsed.

'Hélène,' I said.

'It's me, boss.'

'Your room.'

'Yes.'

I closed my eyes.

'Help me get him upstairs, half-wit!'

Such elegance. It's catching. People always rise to great heights in a crisis.

'Feeling better?' said Hélène, bending over me.

'Yes. You're a great girl, Hélène.'

'I'm quite a good nurse. This time they really did a fine job on you.'

'Just the usual. But I wasn't quite over the last session.'

'How did it happen?'

'Tell you later.'

'That's right. Rest now.'

She went and sat on a chair with a book. I looked at the ceiling, then at the walls. At the idiotic daub of a picture, and the mirror over the mantelpiece.

'A good thing you kept the room on,' I said after a while. She smiled.

'Detective's intuition.'

'It's nice. Well, not bad. For a hotel room. You've left your mark on it.'

'Rest.'

'Funny thing – I've got a feeling I've seen it before.'

'Hotel rooms are all alike.'

'Just the same . . . '

'Boss, please! You must rest your head.'

'My God!' I exclaimed. 'I know this room!'

'You must have brought one of your little bits of fluff here.'

'I prefer a better class of place for my indiscretions.'

'The Transocean, for example . . . '

Then I started to laugh.

'How stupid of me! I'd forgotten this was the hotel in the rue de Valois. I recognized the room because it's the one Lheureux was staying in! After he left it was the only one free, so they gave it to you. That's all. I've been cudgelling my brains over nothing.'

'Talking of Lheureux . . . ' said Hélène.

'Yes?'

'Reboul rang.'

'And?'

'No change.'

'Good. Good old Lheureux . . . '

I shut my eyes and let my thoughts wander.

'He had loads of money on him. Loads. Just ask daft Albert downstairs – he helped himself to some of it. Two wallets he had, Lheureux – one he carried on him, the other one was in his case. The case burst open. Wallet, underpants . . . '

'Rest. You're delirious.'

I kept still for a bit, then went on more quietly.

'The case burst open. Everything fell out. Wallet, underpants, shirts, socks, handkerchiefs . . . The cops took the case away. They must have opened it too. And they're real snoopers. Money, lots of money, underpants, socks . . . Hélène!'

'Yes.'

'There's something wrong.'

'With your head?'

'No, with my thinking. And yet I'm sure I should be on the right track . . . He acted tough. Not like . . . '

'Rest. I'll give you an aspirin.'

'No, I don't want one . . . He had a drink, but he

didn't offer me one. (To hell with him!) . . . He was standing in front of the mirror . . . '

I looked in the mirror . . .

Lheureux emerged from the depths of the mirror and began to pack his case, which was lying open on the bed. He was wearing a sober dark jacket and striped trousers like a floorwalker. His hat was pulled down to shade his eyes from the light, though there was only one weak bulb hanging from the middle of the ceiling. The room smelled of cigars. He had a cigar butt in his mouth still. 'Making tracks?' I said. 'Going home?' 'Looks like it,' he answered. His voice was slightly blurred. 'Emilie will be pleased.' 'Yeah.' He stuffed some more clothes in the case . . . shirts . . . socks . . . 'A nice trick you played on me just now,' I said. He grinned. 'Never mind, I'll add it to your wife's bill.' 'Do that!' He grinned again. I yawned. 'Right,' I said. 'Goodbye, Lheureux. I'm supposed to pack you off home, so I won't delay your departure.' 'Goodbye,' he said, turning to refill his glass. He didn't offer me a drink. Then he vanished into the mirror, on the way to his accident. The case containing the socks, the shirts, and the bulging wallet which Albert helped himself to, remained on the bed for a moment, then it too disappeared.

Whether from drink or from fever, my feet twitched of their own accord.

'It must be staring me in the face,' I said aloud.

'Off again, are you?' said Hélène. 'I might have known you couldn't keep quiet for more than five minutes. I think I'd better call a doctor. One of your friends . . . '

'I don't want a doctor, Hélène – I want a drink.'

'There isn't any. I've only got some surgical spirit. I'll give you an aspirin.'

She went to get a glass of water.

'Hélène,' I said, 'what's that picture?'

'What picture?'

'That awful daub that isn't even hanging straight on the wall.'

'Just an awful daub, as you say.'

'Not by Raphael, by any chance?'

'Leave Raphael out of it.'

'I would if I could, but he insists.'

'Here's some water to wash your aspirin down.'

I pushed the glass aside.

'When you've looked at yourself in the glass. Go on.'

'Mustn't contradict the patient . . . There, I'm looking at myself in the glass.'

'Pretty, eh? You'd be even prettier without—. Oh well . . . How's it fixed, that mirror?'

'It's on a cord hanging from a hook. Come to think of it, this is a pretty lousy room. That's no way to hang a mirror.'

'Stand on a chair and see if it's safe.'

'And meanwhile you leer at my legs, is that it? You *must* be feeling better!'

'Yes to both questions.'

She stood on a chair.

'Dusty?'

'Very.'

'Stop slandering the room. It's fit for a princess. Is the cord new?'

'No. But the ends are very long.'

'As if someone had recently angled the mirror closer to the wall?'

'Could be.'

'Thank you. You can come down now. Lift your skirt up a bit so I get my money's worth.'

Naturally she came down as chastely as possible. Some girls will never understand. I got out of bed, and despite her protests climbed on the chair. I looked pretty fetching myself in my pants and loose shirt. I unhooked the cord, lifted the glass away from the wall, felt behind it and brought out what looked like a piece of thick canvas. It was rough on one side. On the other side too, but that was pleasant to look at. Colourful, pretty, and not too big. About eighteen inches by nine.

'My God!' said Hélène.

'Pass the surgical spirit. I'm going to drink the lot.'

Too stunned to do anything else, she handed me the bottle. I raised it to my lips.

'To your very good health, Raphael,' I said.

I was trembling like a leaf.

15 *The first corpse . . .*
and the rest

'Good old Lheureux!' I laughed.

I was back lying down again. Hélène stood by the bed. She was dressed to go out, with her hat on and a parcel under her arm.

'Whoever would have thought it!' she said for the umpteenth time. 'Lheureux! It was the harmless, insignificant Lheureux who—?'

'I'll tell you all about it later. But for the time being I'll just point out that in this very street the place where Houdini had his theatre is opposite the office of the Ministry of Fine Arts. Art and conjuring. What a coincidence, eh? But *I*'ve produced something rather better than a rabbit out of the mirror. Three million francs, Hélène, if Florimond Faroux is a man of his word. If not, I'll flog the thing to Corbigny . . . '

But suddenly I shivered. I'd been in a dream. I'd forgotten that while I was lying here being looked after . . .

'Corbigny!' I said. 'If he's still alive . . . Has there been any news from Zavatter this afternoon?'

'No.'

'Hell, I must get moving.'

'You've had it for today. Take this tablet. It'll calm you down.'

'Later. So – are you clear what you have to do?'

'Yes. I go to my mother's and hide this parcel in a cupboard she opens only once in a blue moon.'

'Perfect. See you tomorrow.'

'About Lheureux—'

'Later on. I'll tell you later on.'

'But *I've* got something to tell *you*. You were too seedy for me to tell you before. Reboul rang the office not long ago. But not to say progress was still satisfactory. To tell you that this afternoon Lheureux disappeared from the hospital.'

I left the hotel ten minutes after Hélène, wrapped up in Octave Miret's duffel-coat. I still wasn't up to turning cartwheels, but I could walk straight without difficulty and my head was almost back to normal. If I looked at my feet the pavement no longer seemed to leap up in my face. If I had a pastis in my stomach and a pistol under my arm, I'd still be able to cause a few fireworks.

So first I dropped in at the agency. No cop in the street, no suspect caller waiting outside the door, lurking on the stairs or skulking in the office. I had a swig of the medicine I'd had in mind, changed my shirt, picked up my artillery, put the duffel-coat on again, and set off through the calm and chilly night for the Transocean.

I slipped past the reception desk with a patronizing wave at the night porter, and made for the lifts. By the time he'd started to wonder, I'd reached the fourth floor. There I got out of the lift and went up to the fifth on foot. The corridors were only dimly lit, and as I went past one of the rooms I could hear snoring. When I got to Geneviève's room I bent down and put my ear to the keyhole. I could hear muffled voices. I took out a little tool which I use to clean my pipe and which is also handy for absent-minded folk who lose their keys. The lock yielded as quickly as a woman of easy virtue, but with less noise. Inside the front door there was a tiny hall designed to deaden sounds from the corridor, with an inner door leading into the main room. The inner door was usually kept shut, but this being my lucky day it was now open, and the couple inside saw me enter.

Geneviève was lying back in her chair, wearing a dress – an undress, more like – that I hadn't seen before. Clinging. Low necked. Oodles of oomph. But Geneviève wasn't looking her best. Her hair was dishevelled, her make-up sketchy, her eyes red with crying.

The man had been sitting down when I came in, but he stood up politely to greet me. He was about fifty, with harsh and rather heavy features, ill-shaven, with a big black moustache and a good head of hair showing only a few streaks of silver. He was wearing a sober dark jacket, and striped trousers like a floorwalker. I thought he looked rather ill at ease in this get-up – but perhaps that was because I knew they weren't his. One leg was obviously damaged and giving him pain. With his left hand he leaned on a heavy stick. In his right he held an automatic of burnished steel, giving off glints of a very poetic blue.

My lucky day. I should have got out my own gun before I tackled the lock. But it was too late now. Might as well pass it off with a grin and a shrug of the shoulders. What had I got to lose?

I walked into the sitting room.

'Hallo, Larpent!' I said.

*

'Don't come too close, Burma,' he advised. 'Go and stand in the corner and don't move. And put your hands behind your head, if you don't mind.'

I did mind. It hurt. But I didn't say anything, and put my hands behind my head.

'I'm still not very strong,' the other went on. 'Not strong at all.'

Moving with difficulty because of his dicky leg, he moved back and leaned against the wall, covering Geneviève and me with his gun. While he was alone with the woman he'd been sitting down. Now I was there he wanted to be ready for any eventuality.

'No, I'm still not myself,' he said. 'If I knew who the swine was who skittled me in his lousy old jalopy—'

'That's funny,' I interrupted.

'What?'

'For a consideration I can find him for you. I'm a detective.'

'Not for much longer.'

I shrugged, and smiled at Geneviève.

'Hallo, darling.'

She looked at me wildly for a moment, then buried her head in her arms and burst into sobs. She flung herself around as if she was about to have hysterics, and I could see that her stockings were edged with lace and held up with diamanté suspenders. Larpent swore at his mistress in a low and insulting manner.

'Belt up,' I said.

'Poor fool,' he sneered.

Geneviève gradually calmed down. When she raised her head her face was still bathed in tears. I nodded – ouch! – towards the table, where a copy of the *Crépu* lay open at the famous article.

'I told you so, darling,' I said to her. 'It was a load of crap. It was that that brought our jealous friend here. When he read the article, in hospital, he wondered what it signified. He might be imagining things, but he wanted to be sure. So he escaped, though he still wasn't fit to be discharged. He went and got himself a gun, and some false whiskers in case he met any of the staff in the hotel – a ghost would have caused rather a fuss. And by way of further precaution, he must have got in here through a service entrance. Am I right, Larpent?'

'Mind your own business.'

Geneviève suddenly stood up. The man levelled the blue barrel of the gun at her.

'I want to go,' she wailed. 'Let me go!'

'Sit down!' barked Larpent.

'Hey, Houdini!' I said. 'What are we supposed to do? You're not going to keep us here for ever?'

He shrugged disdainfully.

'I'm leaving. And leaving you two behind. Dead. I can't afford to turn my back on you, wounded like this. I'll arrange it all very carefully. Tragic lovers. Suicide pact. I'll arrange it *very* carefully.'

'Right. You shoot us, then you leave. Then what?'

'Never you mind.'

'Then you'll go and collect your picture, and you'll sell it and go and live abroad.'

'Exactly.'

'No, monsieur.'

'What?'

'I said no. "Monsieur" was a slip of the tongue. The picture isn't behind the mirror any more, Larpent.'

I thought he'd have to shoot me – he wouldn't be

able to contain himself. The big gun shook in his hand. I feared the worst.

'My God, Burma! Say that again!'

'The picture isn't behind the mirror any more.'

He made a superhuman effort and pulled himself together.

'Where is it then?'

'If you want to know that you'll have to let Geneviève and me go. But I warn you – I've got the feeling the picture's lost a lot of its value in the last few days. With so many bodies lying around it'll be hard to find a buyer. After about four corpses the thing gets a bit risky. But I'll let you have old Raphael in exchange for our two lives. What do I care about Raphael? Frédéric Delanglade and Oscar Dominguez are my friends. Raphael – don't make me laugh!'

'You're talking bilge!'

'You're a tough guy, are you, Larpent? No flies on you? You're right. I *was* talking bilge. I said the picture isn't behind the mirror any more. I might just as well have said it isn't behind Notre-Dame.'

'To hell with Notre-Dame!'

'That's all right by me – I'm an atheist, anyway. So, it was a lie. And the fact that there were a couple of twins so alike they could deceive anyone who didn't know them very well or see them both together – that's another lie, eh? Shall I tell you a few more?'

He raised an eyebrow.

'And I took you for a sucker! . . . Tell me all you know, Burma. Then I'll know if you're bluffing about the mirror.'

'If you like – you know it's true already. But I don't mind showing off, especially with ladies present.'

I gave Geneviève a smile both affectionate and sad.

'Well, these twin brothers were crooks. They came from a place that was wiped off the map in the 1914-18 war, so there were no inconvenient records. A cinch. Whenever the police thought a villain called Daumas was in one place, he'd pop up in another like a will-o'-the-wisp. You were smarter than your brother – he's the one who got himself rubbed out, after all. But your brother may have been luckier in love. You both hankered after a girl called Aurélienne, but if either of you slept with her it wasn't you. I could be wrong about all that, but I need some sort of rivalry between the two of you to explain *your* actions. Because, if you don't mind my saying so in the friendliest possible manner, you'd be an indescribable louse if you'd killed your own brother without the excuse that you hated him for some reason or other. Right. So one day the two brothers part. I presume you go on living off some form of high-class swindling and having the devil's own luck, while your brother retires to the provinces under the name of Lheureux. His background is rather mysterious, but that's of no consequence. One day he makes a break for it and comes up to Paris. His wife, who's an invalid, employs me to send him back COD. I find him and we become friends. The sight of me often seems to amuse him; he's laughing up his sleeve. After all, a former criminal, perhaps a criminal still, being protected by a detective . . . He finds it so funny he does another bunk the following year, and this time it's he who lets me know about it. We go on the town together. And now here we are in 1954. This time, instead of in the summer, he absconds in January. And he doesn't phone up to tell me about it. I presume . . . '

Larpent sighed.

'You do a lot of presuming, don't you?'

'It's my job, old boy. So I presume you'd got in contact with him again, assuming – you see I can assume as well as presume – assuming you weren't in contact with one another all the time. And you suggested he should join you in a certain project. I'm put on his track for the third time by Mme Lheureux, and run him to ground in a restaurant near Les Halles. He doesn't seem very pleased to see me, and gives me the slip – he has an appointment with you nearby in connection with the famous project. A fatal project as far as he's concerned. You both go down into the cellar in the rue Pierre-Lescot, and hey presto! no more Louis Lheureux. A couple of bullets have killed and partially disfigured him. You needed an unfrequented place like that so that you could exchange clothes with him undisturbed. But afterwards you lose no time in getting to a phone and calling the police. Why? Because it was necessary for the body to be found quickly, and found with the forged Raphael on it. The idea was that everyone should think that Larpent was dead, and that he'd been mixed up in the theft from the Louvre. And who was this principally aimed at? Your own accomplices. You'd been meaning to get rid of them for a long time . . . '

'More supposition.'

'Maybe. But it's no mere supposition that you had the genuine painting, and intended to lie low until the buyer Octave Miret was angling for turned up. Then, when you'd pocketed a hundred or so million francs, you were going to disappear. It would have been a hundred or so million, or even more, in case you didn't know.'

'Don't you worry!' Larpent laughed. 'However much

it is, I'm not going to let it slip through my fingers!'

'That's as may be . . . Anyhow, once the deed is done, you hurry to Lheureux's hotel in the rue de Valois. I presume, if you'll allow me, that you'd got your brother to tell you all about his relationship with me. And the poor fish, just a few moments before his death, had described our encounter in the restaurant. So when I come upon you packing the case in his room, you act as if you know me, but speak as little as possible and get rid of me as fast as you can. But my visit bothers you, and you feel you'd better not carry the painting about with you after all. You put it behind the mirror, and fix the mirror closer to the wall. No one will disturb it there until you find it convenient to come and collect it. And should you meet anyone undesirable, you won't have anything incriminating about you – you've already got rid of the gun you used to shoot Lheureux with. So off you go. And you don't meet any*one* undesirable, but you do run into a car. You were lucky really – if the cops had found the picture in your case they'd have packed you off to a cell instead of to a hospital ward.'

'Maybe. But it spoiled everything. If I knew who that swine was—'

'Give me a thousand francs and I'll give you a hint. No? Stingy fellow. With more than a hundred million practically in your pocket . . . Oh well . . . Just this once, by way of advertisement, ladies and gentlemen, M. Larpent and Mlle Geneviève . . . '

She turned pale.

'Not for a thousand francs, nor for a hundred, but free, gratis and for nothing, I'll tell you who it was who was driving that car. It was me. Nestor Burma. The detective who can KO any mystery.'

'That's right – laugh, you son of a bitch.' Larpent's voice was shaking with repressed hatred.

'I saw you were trying to escape. I suspected, though I wasn't absolutely sure, that you weren't Lheureux. And I'd seen the dead body in the banana shop. So I wanted to keep you handy, without letting the police in on the affair, because I had an idea there might be a profitable mystery underneath all this carry-on if I could only manage to KO it. Everything pointed to you as the murderer. By denting you a bit I could immobilize a valuable commodity for a while without actually destroying it.'

'Laugh while you can!'

'But while you're champing at the bit in your hospital bed your accomplices get going. They think you're really dead – but who could have done it? They think straight away of your mistress – but we'll come back to that. Birikos and Chassard, that ideal couple, think at first that I'm the go-between, and search my office for clues. They find a letter and fight over it . . . Oh, I was forgetting – they also find a photograph of Lheureux, which they take to be a photograph of you. They deduce that I know Larpent and am in cahoots with him . . . The letter doesn't get them very far, but they fight to the death for it. Exit M. Nick Birikos, who, by the way, would never have cuckolded you, unlike the ambidextrous Chassard. *He*, whether or no he really believes Geneviève killed you to get the picture, chances his arm with her – he's fed up with old women . . . and old men. But he makes a mess of it, and Geneviève calls me in.'

Larpent, still leaning stiffly on his stick, still aiming his automatic at us, gave a bitter laugh.

'Ha ha,' he sneered.

'Funnier than you think . . . *I* slept with her.'

'Funnier still.'

I didn't like his vulgar guffaw.

'Stow it, Larpent,' I snapped.

'OK, go on.'

'I've nearly finished. Geneviève and I make the mistake of not kicking Chassard out for good and all. She thinks he's not as bad as all that. With the result that, on the pretence of providing her with some publicity, he gets the charming little nitwit . . . ' I turned to Geneviève. 'Sorry, darling . . . He gets the little dear to agree to publishing a sensational article. And why does he do that? Because he says to himself: the papers haven't said anything about the relationship between her and Larpent, and if the bloke who wants to buy the picture, who must be pretty distraught, sees the article, he'll go and see Geneviève. Then, Chassard thinks, *he*'ll manage to get the cash out of the purchaser without giving him anything in exchange. The buyer didn't show up, but the article did make *you* see red, and you rushed round to give the lady a piece of your mind. Her face must have been a picture when she saw you blow in.'

'It was!'

'Naturally. You were supposed to be dead.'

There was a pause.

'Is that all?' said Larpent.

'Yes.'

'The super detective, eh?'

'At your service, Houdini.'

'You don't know the half of it.'

'Too bad. I've said enough, anyway – I'm tired, and my tongue's hanging out for a drink. You haven't got anything that would help, have you, Geneviève?'

She slowly shook her head, smiling at me affectionately. Her eyes brimmed with tears.

'My darling,' she said.

'Right, Larpent,' I said briskly. 'Let's go and get the picture.'

'Don't move!' he snarled.

He tottered slightly on his injured leg. The gun quivered.

'Bastards!' he said.

Then all hell broke loose.

He fired at Geneviève, but missed. For a second or two, though, he'd taken his eyes off me. I whipped out my gun and shot him in the leg, the good one. My lucky day. I missed. He aimed at my middle, his pistol belching flames, the recoil obviously adding to his pain. From Geneviève there came a dreadful cry, and she sprang forward and fell at my feet, clutching as if in a last amorous gesture the breasts whose ageing she'd so dreaded. She'd torn her dress open as she leaped forward to protect me, and I could see a diamanté suspender pressing against her thigh and glittering in the flash of the detonations.

I had met her cry with a howl of grief. So many things had suddenly died. Then I set my jaw and let Larpent have it. After his gun had gone silent I was still emptying mine into him. At last mine fell silent too.

Beside myself with pain and rage, I went over to him. He was still breathing. Good – let Faroux and his men take delivery of him alive, and let him die on the way to gaol. Above all, let him die.

Fifty million, a hundred million, all the millions there are! Filthy money – it louses up everything!

I bent over Geneviève, picked her up and went and laid her on her bed. Some of her blood came off on my hands. It was only yesterday that I'd slept with her. She slowly raised one hand, with its long slender fingers, to her heaving, bloodstained bosom. The broken nail on the forefinger hadn't had time to grow. Her lips moved feebly.

'My darling,' she said.

16 Low again

I looked at myself in the glass in the sitting room. Nestor Burma, super detective. Grey-faced, unshaven, dishevelled. Almost alone. Alone at last, as they say. They'd all gone now. The hotel officials and staff; Florimond Faroux and his men. I'd provided the Superintendent with an abridged version of the story: the complete showdown could come later. The law had carried off the lawbreaker. With all those bullets in him he'd rattle all the way to the hospital. He was no more fit to be moved than Geneviève was, but they didn't spare him the journey. He was a crook. They had nothing against her. They were doing all they could for her in the bedroom – a doctor and two nurses, all in white. They might just as well have gone home. It was all over. Nestor Burma, the super 'tec. Standing dishevelled in front of the glass, his mouth full of dust and ashes.

The phone broke into these gloomy thoughts.

Faroux.

'He was some guy, Larpent.'

'Was?'

'He's dead. It was only to be expected. You certainly went for him! No one must touch your lady love, eh? . . . There's still a mystery about Birikos's death, because Larpent was in hospital the night the Greek was killed . . . but still . . . We found another gun, that hadn't been used this evening, in Larpent's pocket. And what do you think? It was the very same gun that killed Birikos. *And* a couple of other blokes in the Palais-Royal early this evening. I don't know if you knew about that.'

'No.'

'Well, it was Larpent who bumped them off. He was out of hospital by then. One of the victims was an antique dealer called Miret. The other was a young man by the name of Chassard with no visible means of support. That Larpent was a real killer.'

'It was Chassard who got Geneviève to agree to that article.'

'A nasty piece of work, eh? As for Mlle Levasseur, I think we had quite the wrong idea about her at first . . . In spite of her courage tonight, she's really more of a little scatterbrain than anything.'

'That's right. A little scatterbrain.'

'How is she?'

'As well as anyone can be when they're plugged full of lead.'

'Hmm . . . Well, goodbye, Burma.'

'Goodbye.'

I hung up.

A little scatterbrain!

I went into the other room. The night-light by the bed left Geneviève's face in shadow. One of the nurses came silently to meet me.

'Do you want to speak to her?'

'Is that possible?'

'Everything is possible.'

I went over to the bed. She sensed I was there. She opened her eyes. Huge hollow eyes in her lovely bloodless face. She gave me a piteous smile. She looked like a hunted animal. I took her hand.

'Superintendent Faroux just phoned. It was Larpent who killed Miret and Chassard.'

'I wasn't worth it,' she breathed.

I pressed her hand and said nothing.

'It was because I was afraid of growing old,' she said.

'Yes, Geneviève.'

I went back into the sitting room, shut the door behind me, switched out the lights and opened the windows. The cold air did me good. Day was a long time coming. I filled my pipe but stood there without lighting it.

Little scatterbrain! Innocent little scatterbrain! . . .

When Larpent, pretending to be Lheureux, came out of the hotel in the rue de Valois, who was waiting, in the convertible I missed by inches, to drive him to a safe hiding place? Geneviève. Geneviève, who hadn't hesitated to give away the secret of her liaison with Larpent in order to be able to 'identify' Lheureux's body as his. She was Larpent's accomplice. She was supposed to run away with him and the money. What had happened at the Transocean tonight showed that Larpent mightn't have kept their agreement. But there had *been* an agreement between them. Geneviève felt herself getting old, and she wanted lots of money, and quickly. As if money could ward off age. Madness! She saw the accident, found out what hospital Larpent had been taken to, and went there early the next morning and charmed her way in to see him before Reboul came on duty. Larpent must have asked her to write to Miret, getting him to wait. She typed the letter herself, making lots of mistakes and breaking a nail in the process. He must also have told her to sound me out somehow; the oldest and best-tried method was still the most effective. He'd never told her where the picture was, but she knew who the accomplices were. She also knew the identity of the go-between, which they did not. Chassard, thinking I was the go-between, supplied her with a pretext for contacting me without arousing anyone's suspicion. The scene in which he 'bothered' her was an act put on specially for my benefit.

At that point a snag occured. Without giving up her desire for the rejuvenating millions, Geneviève was suddenly smitten – as I was – by a new, violent, and irresistible attraction. She'd meant to lure me into a trap so as to find out what I was up to, but gave it up. So then another plan, thought up by Chassard in case the Delilah plot failed, was put into operation. The newspaper article! She now dropped Larpent, and concentrated on getting her hands on the fortune to be provided by the unknown buyer. The *Crépu* article was supposed to raise him. Miret was left out of this: Chassard didn't know who he was; Geneviève didn't want to pump him and thus bring him into it unless Covet's piece failed to produce the desired result.

But Miret, on the other hand, wanted to get in touch with Geneviève, to pump *her* for any information she might have as mistress of the 'dead' Larpent. Miret was the aged beau in the bar at the *Cricket*, and it was I who, during my conversation with him, gave them all the name and address of the buyer, Corbigny. She knocked me out with her perfume, but couldn't bring herself to kill me. (Miret and Chassard weren't so lucky. They were probably killed because they were inconvenient witnesses.) Just as I couldn't bring myself to kill her.

I wondered if she'd been to visit the *Sunflower*. If so,

it must have been in vain. And it must have been tonight – the night now slowly ending. Larpent, having skipped from the hospital, had come to the Transocean not because the newspaper article made him jealous but because it made him think she was trying to double-cross him. And to be on the safe side he took charge of the revolver with which she'd murdered the two men she now accused *him* of killing, in the Palais-Royal.

The sky over Paris was slowly lightening.

She was dying in the next room. No one would ever know what she'd done. Larpent's name could easily bear the weight of her crimes. The name of the elegant model from the Place Vendôme was safe. The public would mourn a lovely woman shot down in a luxurious hotel suite by an international criminal. No one but I would know she'd died protecting with that warm, tender, scented body the body of a hard-up private eye who smelled of tobacco.

But perhaps, like her, like everyone, I was imagining things.

I felt exhausted, broken. She was dying in the next room.

Someone touched me on the shoulder. I turned round. The nurse. I didn't say anything. She didn't say anything either – it was all in her eyes. I turned, went out on to the balcony, and stood and watched the dawn break over Paris.

The sun was rising behind the Louvre.

Paris, 1954

Other books by Léo Malet

The Rats of Montsouris £3.99

'Then, slowly, without quite knowing why, I retraced my steps. Was it because of the redhead or because of the man with the tattoo? I think on the whole, it was because of the redhead . . . '

A rendezvous with a fellow ex-POW leads Nestor Burma, dynamic chief of the Fiat Lux Detective Agency, to a dimly lit bar in the rue du Moulin-de-la-Vierge. A venue quite empty of both windmills and virgins . . .

What he finds there is his tattooed mate, now part of a gang of burgulars called the Rats of Montsouris. But this particular Rat is on to something so big he can only trust Burma. And when someone betrays him, the question remains - what *are* the back streets of the 14th arrondissement hiding?

Burma, assisted by the beautiful Hélène, is in for a string of seedy surprises . . .

120 rue de la Gare   £3.99

*'We'd arrived in Lyon, Lyon-Perrache station to be precise. It was
two o'clock by my watch and I had a nasty taste in my mouth . . . '*

Nestor Burma has seen a lot of strange men die in his time. So
when a soldier without a name utters the dying words "120 rue de la
Gare", the chief of the famous Fiat Lux Detective Agency is only mildy
intrigued.

It's when a colleague meets death gasping the same phrase that
Burma's interest – and fury – are fully aroused. Time to take out his
pipe, discover the secret of the morbid address and nail the murderer
in one fell swoop.

One problem. Where *is* 120 rue de la Gare?

fluttered to and fro, crashing into one another, squawking and screeching at the tops of their voices, no doubt more frightened than delighted by their sudden freedom. Never mind, they'd learn. Come on, pals! No more bars, no more skimpy perches, no more idiots whistling and poking dirty fingers at you! I flung the shop door open wide and waved my arms encouragingly. This way! Come on! The birds streamed out like a long multicoloured scarf, and the kids gathered round Hélène on the other side of the street jumped up and down for joy by the river. Their cheers rose up among the trills with which the birds rediscovered the brisk, reviving, inexhaustible air.

Peltier moaned and tore his hair, but it didn't occur to him for a moment to call the cops. The birds scattered over the Paris sky as it was briefly lit up by a burst of sun. Peltier groaned. The swings still rocked gently to and fro inside the empty cages.

I went over to Hélène. Her lovely grey eyes brimmed with tears of delight.

But there was no point in deluding ourselves. It had been a nice little interlude, but I had a strong feeling the nastiness was about to start up again.

to lend him your premises to stow me away. And let me tell you I don't like that at all.'

His face went the same colour as his overalls. Dirty white.

'Listen,' he whined. 'Yes, he did want to use the room at the back of the shop. I couldn't refuse. I didn't know – I didn't *ask* him what for. I just gave him the keys. And afterwards I found them left in the door – just think, I might have been burgled! But I hadn't any idea what it was all about, M. Burma. I hadn't, I swear!'

'I still don't like it. Birikos was a wrong 'un. At least, that's the conclusion I came to from his behaviour to me. And for all I know you may be a wrong 'un, too. And the police may be interested to hear that you lent Birikos your place to imprison, bind and gag a private detective. What do you think, bird man? You look like a dying duck.'

'Are you . . . are you going to call the police?'

'You don't like the idea of being shut up in a cage, eh? Did you ask your birds if *they* were keen on it? . . . Don't worry, I'm *not* going to call the cops. That's not my style. You weren't with Birikos when he searched my office, and you didn't kill him. You were just the left luggage office. That doesn't concern the police – it's just between you and me. If the police do come it'll be because *you*'ve called them. And if you do call them, I'll tell all.'

I pointed to a large aviary full of little birds.

'What are they?'

'Goldfinches.'

Suddenly he understood, and tried to jump me. I brushed him aside.

'Go on, Peltier – call the cops. If you've got the cheek!'

I opened all the cages one after the other. The whole shop filled with the rush of wings. Birds of all shapes and sizes